feels like home

Sophie —

Rock the word and be heard)!

— Trujillo

2010

ALSO BY e.E. CHARLTON-TRUJILLO

Prizefighter en Mi Casa

e.E. Charlton-Trujillo

feels
like
home

DELACORTE PRESS

Published by Delacorte Press
an imprint of Random House Children's Books
a division of Random House, Inc.
New York

www.randomhouse.com/teens

Educators and librarians, for a variety of teaching tools,
visit us at www.randomhouse.com/teachers

Library of Congress Cataloging-in-Publication Data
Charlton-Trujillo, e. E.
Feels like home / by e. E. Charlton-Trujillo.— 1st ed.
p. cm.
Summary: Following the death of her father, seventeen-year-old Michelle's older brother—who had disappeared six years earlier—returns to their small Texas town where, with the help of S.E. Hinton's *The Outsiders*, the two siblings try to find a way to move beyond a past tragedy.
ISBN 978-0-385-73332-8 (trade) — ISBN 978-0-385-90349-3 (glb)
[1. Brothers and sisters—Fiction. 2. Grief—Fiction. 3. Conduct of life—Fiction. 4. City and town life—Fiction. 5. Family problems—Fiction.] I. Title.
PZ7.C381855Sta 2007
[E]—dc22   2006000275

The text of this book is set in 12-point Baskerville MT.

Book design by Angela Carlino

Printed in the United States of America

10 9 8 7 6 5 4 3 2 1

First Edition

Dedicated to my brother
May you always find your way home . . .

feels like home

1

When I stepped out into the bright sunlight from the darkness of the movie house, I had only two things on my mind: Paul Newman and a ride home.

My brother and I read the opening of S. E. Hinton's *The Outsiders* every single day back then no matter where we left off. Before the accident anyway. I was in seventh grade and he was in twelfth and as far as I was concerned it was better than anything I'd ever heard. Not saying that I had heard a lot, but that didn't matter 'cause Danny read it and made it sound more special than anything in Three Rivers, Texas, population 4,043.

Better than swirly-tipped ice cream cones from the Dairy Queen or greasy Personal Pans from the Pizza Hut. Better than the maroon Chuck Taylor basketball Converse he got me for Christmas or the souped-up '76 ash and chrome Chevy he grease-monkeyed for six months, just so he could drive me two hundred miles to band camp. Even though his name shot out the mouths of every person in town at the state football finals his senior year, he said it was my voice he heard over all of them. Me, his kid sister, Mickey, who he'd made sure was sitting on the bench with the cheerleaders at every game. He never left me alone. Not for a girl, not for anything. That's when Danny was gold.

But when there wasn't a crowd. When there wasn't the town doting on Danny, or him and Roland preparing their speeches for the Heisman Trophy or all the energy around the first state football victory in thirty-two years, it really was the two of us. And whenever Danny bent back the binding of that yellow-paged *Outsiders*, we both belonged to something that felt like home and that meant a lot 'cause ours hadn't for some time.

I hadn't thought of any of that in years. But for some reason, in the sweltering heat of the gravesite, it was all I could think of. . . .

"Ashes to ashes. Dust to dust . . . ," said Minister Howard.

Because the onetime hero turned prodigal misfit—

"So that's really him?" my best friend, Christina, whispered, wiping her streaking mascara.

Had come home.

Somehow Danny Owens, the brother I'd tried to forget, had found his way back after six years of nothing.

2

He pushed through the crowd alongside the tent and made his way to the front, inches from the casket. Shallow sprays of straw-colored sunlight tiptoed along his mess of unwrangled chestnut hair. His busted-up faded Levi's had given up on any kind of shaping and frayed along the dirt-stained cuffs. Danny was a hard sharp edge at twenty-four and held himself stiff as the tent pole beside him. Nothing like the full-of-hope, anything-is-possible guy I grew up with before all the trouble. But he looked pretty much the way he did that night he disappeared, so for the life of me I couldn't imagine why he'd come back—especially for Dad's funeral. But there he was, across from me and half the town he'd destroyed, with his dark dry eyes fixed on Dad's casket.

People began to whisper. Chatter. Their voices buzzed behind me, sitting in the front row, like a swarm of gnats quickly clustering around my damp ears. When I turned around and looked at Mr. Jimenez, one of Dad's AA buddies, he nudged the woman beside him to hush up. A nudge wasn't going to settle something like Danny back in town. Not that I cared one bit if it made him uneasy, standing there like he'd shown up to a party he wasn't invited to but decided to stay anyway. I just didn't want it all to start up again at the funeral. Dad deserved better than that.

Uncle Jack put his hand on my knee. Giving me that look he was so good at. The one that asked "You okay?" I'd learned to be okay. I had to be.

Christina joined in with what most of the women had been doing. Desperately fanning their faces with their hands or scraps of mail pulled from their purses to salvage their caked-on melting makeup. Men loosened up their ties or

3

wafted their polyester jackets, releasing a nauseating combo of body odor and cheap cologne. The dress I'd borrowed from Christina, 'cause I never had a need for one, clung damp and tired from the South Texas humidity. It was like the moment Danny stepped to the front of the crowd the temperature went up twenty degrees, and the smell of smoke slithered between each and every one of us, prying its boneless body into every sweat-filled pore.

Minister Howard finished his piece. People made their way to the casket to pay their final respects. And Danny ducked under the tent skirt, weaving through the crowd, keeping his head low. Unbelievable.

"What's he doing here?" I asked Uncle Jack, whose eyes followed Danny.

"I'll be right back, Mickey."

And there he went chasing after him. Just like he useta.

Minister Howard shook hands as he made his way to me. I'd somehow managed to avoid him until right then. Not that he was a bad man, but Dad and I hadn't necessarily been the churchgoing type. Still, it was Minister Howard's basement where they held the Wednesday night AA meetings, and I guess he felt it was somehow his moral duty to speak at Dad's funeral. Or so it was told to me by Uncle Jack.

"Let the church know if you need anything, Michelle." Minister Howard smiled what must've been heartfelt, but I couldn't feel it. "We can't always understand moments like this, but your father is in a better place now. Heaven is the kingdom of delight."

I didn't smile back, which I think was the expected gesture. Just about anywhere outside of Three Rivers would've seemed a better place from what I always figured. But heaven just wasn't on Dad's to do list when he left the house Monday morning for some car parts he needed from the city. The last thing he said was how he was going to bring home Kentucky Fried Chicken for dinner. He'd wanted it for over a week. Kentucky Fried Chicken and mashed potatoes smothered in creamy white gravy. Gravy we'd have to make ourselves but that was fine 'cause it was something we could do together. And he always brought those—those Little Bucket Parfaits for dessert. . . .

Was he thinking about that when—

"How you doing, Mickey?" Albert Trevino said, sitting in Uncle Jack's empty seat.

He gave me a big brother kind of hug, and I know he must've showered but I could still smell the garage on him. It was a good smell. Like Dad.

"Just let us know," said Minister Howard, still standing there.

I nodded and he made his way out of the tent.

"Thanks," I told Albert. "I didn't know what to say to him."

"You hanging in there?" asked Albert.

"I'm okay," I said.

"I see Danny's back."

I shrugged.

"He looks good," said Albert, clearing his throat. "You know, Mickey, I don't gotta tell you your father meant a lot to me. He was kinda like a dad to me too. If you need *anything*, you give me a call. Anytime, okay?"

I nodded.

5

"And don't stop coming around the garage." He rested his hand on my shoulder. "You're my foreign car specialist."

His wife, Priscilla, pregnant as could be without popping out a set of twins right there, stood beside him.

"Hey, Mickey. I'm really sorry, *mijita*," she said, resting her hand on her belly.

"Thanks."

Was I supposed to keep saying that?

"We'll see you at the house," Albert said, getting up.

I hadn't had a chance to even get out of my seat as a line of Dad's AA buddies started shaking hands with me. Each with their "I'm sorry . . . whatever you need . . . just take it one day at a time. . . ."

I looked over at Christina, who had gotten up with one knee on her chair. Peering through the people who were on the outer folds of the tent.

"He looks different," she said.

"Who?"

"Your brother."

"Different than what?" I said, finishing the last of the handshaking.

"I don't know. Than the trophy-case pictures at the high school. And he sure doesn't look the way some people talk about him." She sat back down with one leg under the other. "The evil *gringo* that kept Three Rivers from the fame of a Mexican quarterback in the NFL."

"Yeah, well." I stood, peeling the damp dress away from me. "He is."

"I don't know," she said, following me to Dad's casket.

6

"Just thought he'd look different. You think he's gonna move here?"

"What After School Special are you living in? He won't last the night. This town is like kryptonite to him. Trust me."

"Why do you think he came back then?"

"I don't know and I don't care."

Most everyone had fanned out to their cars. It was just the two of us and Mr. spindly-boned Yanek from the funeral home. Christina did the Catholic cross thing, finishing with a kiss on her immaculate crucifix.

"You want me to wait?" she said. "I'll totally hang out if you want."

"Nah, it's okay. I'm not gonna stay long."

She gave me a strong hug. The kind that said something that you can't figure out how to say in words, especially when you're only seventeen and in uncomfortable shoes.

"You *sure* you don't want to ride with me and Hector?"

I shook my head.

"Okay. See you at your house, Gringa."

I watched her meet up with Hector, the only one of her seven brothers she got along with.

"Michelle," said Mr. Yanek behind dense black sunglasses. "I'm . . . terribly sorry for your loss."

"Thanks," I said, really sick of spitting out the word just for good manners.

"I'll give you a moment." He stepped outside the tent and stood with his back to me.

There I was. Alone with Dad. I put my hand on the casket, trying to imagine him inside. 'Cause it was so hot, just for a second I wondered how he could breathe in there. Then I swallowed real hard like I had a fat greasy piece of barbecue wedged in my throat. Closed my eyes and counted to at least fifteen before I was able to wash down that tension all balled up in there.

The two o'clock train rattled less than fifty feet from the graveyard, howling and rocking the rails as it made its way toward town a couple miles away. My feet slipped in and out of my flats as I walked from beneath the tent. I'd bought them at a Payless in the city off the clearance rack just for the funeral, and they were nearly killing me. Danny hunched behind the wheel of Dad's new fixer-upper truck, resting his chin on his fist. Uncle Jack leaned against the door talking to him. Danny didn't seem to listen. He just aimlessly stared at the dashboard dust.

"Hey, girl," Uncle Jack said, noticing me out the corner of his eye.

I stopped way shy of the truck, so he walked over to me.

"How did Dad's truck get here?" I said.

"I asked Albert to leave it at the Exxon where the Greyhound lets off for Danny—"

"You knew he was coming?"

"I knew he *said* he was coming. I didn't know for sure he'd be here and that's why I didn't say anything to you."

I shook my head.

"Hey."

"What?" I said, not looking at Uncle Jack.

"Just had a few words with him."

"Are those words 'You're leaving'?" I said.

8

"Mickey . . . now, this is hard for him too."

"Doubt it," I said, digging the heel of my shoe in the dirt.

"Give him a chance." Uncle Jack brushed the hair out of my eyes.

He wasn't real family. Uncle Jack. Not in the blood sense. He was Dad's best friend since grade school and I'd called him Uncle Jack as far back as I could remember. The real Owens family lived up in east Texas and didn't want anything to do with us even after Mom split when I was just seven. When I called them about the funeral, they said I had the wrong number and hung up on me before I got a chance to say "I'm sorry."

"Now everyone's headed over to your place, so why don't you ride with him," said Uncle Jack.

"No way. Don't push him off on me."

"He's your brother, Mickey."

I bit the inside of my lip, watching the last of the cars crawl off. Mr. Yanek was under the tent with the gravedigger and some other man as they lowered the coffin into the ground. He raised his head and noticed me watching and quickly had them stop.

"Please," Uncle Jack said. "I'm not going to make you. I just think it's a good thing."

I knew Uncle Jack loved Danny like a son in spite of the fact that Danny hurt a lot of people, and especially Aunt Sara all those years ago. But I was the last one he should've been expecting to march in a welcome home nutcase brother parade.

"He's come a long way for you," said Uncle Jack.

I took a long hard look at Danny, who wasn't looking anywhere near me. I didn't know why he'd come back, but it sure wasn't for me.

"Fine," I said. "But don't expect a family reunion."

I shook my head and headed toward the truck.

The rusty door creak-squeaked as I opened it. I huffed climbing in and before the door shut, the vinyl seat seared the back of my thighs even through the dress. Danny's brow dipped lower than before as he stared out the cracked windshield splattered with yellow bug guts and caliche dust.

"Where you wanna go?" Danny said, still staring off.

I paused for a moment, wondering if it was a trick question.

"Home," I said. "Where else would we go?"

2

I watched Danny through the kitchen window all scrunched up on the rickety rust-speckled swing set out back. A cigarette swirled smoke from between his fingers. He'd been there for over two hours with his boot heels dragging, sometimes making wide U-shaped grooves in the overgrown spring green grass dusted with feather-topped weeds. Sitting on the swing set Mom put together in one of her wild flamboyant moods—one of her better days. One side of it sighed from his weight as he gently twisted back and forth, tangling the chains, then whipping them loose.

Danny made it a point to ditch the crowd gathered on the porch and front yard of our not so roomy three-bedroom house the minute we pulled into the gravel driveway. He didn't say so much as a word. Just shot out of the truck and hopped the chain-link fence with the speed of a stray cat running from a pack of mean-ass kids squeezing fistfuls of rocks.

But right then, everyone had gone except Christina, who stood beside me all wide-eyed.

"I tell you, your brother looks like a superstar." She smacked a mouthful of tortilla. "Maybe he's famous somewhere."

"The only thing Danny's famous for is disappearing," I said.

He took a drag off his cigarette and made it look as cool as James Dean.

"Look at him. I think he looks like one of them *gringos* in the *Tigerbeat–Bop* teen magazines stuck up all over Angie's locker at work."

"Since when do you hang out with Angie?"

"Since never, Gringa. The girl was making her face up last weekend before she went to Shorty's party at the river. She'd heard Ricky was going to be there and all she could do was go on about how she was gonna score."

"Ricky Martinez?"

"The one and only green-eyed Chicano flunkie."

"It was kindergarten."

"Hey, I know you got this—"

"Don't—"

"*Thing* for the Mexican, but if you can't pass citizenship and nap time then I don't even know."

"He's not dumb, Christina."

"Maybe, but he *is* pretty much rich and with the jock

squad. And those guys treat us *only* so well because we actually use our heads instead of spreading our legs like Mary's arms at the church." She crossed herself, kissing her crucifix. "Anyway, that's when I saw all those pictures plastered in Angie's locker. It's really gross considering she's almost twenty."

Christina offered up the mauled remainder of her dripping buttered tortilla. I waved it away.

"You should totally eat. Don't roll your eyes at me, Gringa. You'll get the shakes and you know it."

"I'm fine. Okay?"

"Forget that. Come over here and I'll make you a sandwich," she said, dragging me by my elbow to the table. "So you staying here with him tonight?"

"Right . . . and call me when you're the first Mexican American female president. I told you my brother ain't staying. He'd have to look the word up to figure what it means."

Before she had her hand good inside the bread bag a horn honked.

Christina jogged into the living room and pulled back the curtains, sending a wave of dust into the air. "My mom."

She scratched her head carefully around her foundation.

I hadn't really thought about Christina leaving. Of course she had to, but then what?

"*Ay* . . . I have to—"

"I know," I said.

"So you'll call me later." She slipped into her shoes.

"Yeah." I rolled my toe over the carpet. "I gotta get all this food put up anyway. Not to mention I gotta study for Hodges' history quiz tomorrow."

"Hey, you got a Get Out of Jail Free card. They don't expect you to go to school."

Christina's mom laid on the horn.

"*Ay*, I hear you, Mexican," she shouted at the window. "That woman is impossible. We totally can't be related."

She gave me another one of those big hugs, only that time something made me squeeze and hold just long enough to say I was scared.

"It's gonna be okay," she said with her arms still around me. "And if it's not you can totally call me and cry about it."

She pulled back. Her eyes had watered up.

"*Ay*, Mexican," I said. "You're gonna mess up your face if you start crying again."

She slung her purse embroidered with the Mexican flag over her shoulder.

"You know you can cry now. No one's looking," she said.

The horn wailed again. Christina rolled her eyes and stuck her head out the door. "I'm coming!" She looked back at me. "Later, Gringa. And hey. Eat something."

In a breath she was out the door. She was gone.

I pushed back the curtains and watched her disappear into her mother's black '82 Buick Skylark. We waved to each other as her mother tore out of the driveway. Christina's mother hated that we were best friends. I was white, smart and from a broken home. All of which to Christina's mom kept Christina from being like the other Hispanic girls with her mind on cooking and finding a future husband. Even if she had another year of high school.

"Boys are going to think you are a lesbian only hanging

out with that girl," her mother said to her once. "They won't want anything to do with you then."

Christina laughed and said, "At least I won't be pregnant before graduation."

Her mom didn't think it was funny.

I sank into the couch cushions, looking at the heap of food piled on the dining table. The table that only recently Dad and I had started to make into something like families on TV. Every other Sunday since the end of March, he'd grill up hamburgers, Magic Burgers he called them, or steaks on the pit out back. When we didn't come inside, we'd sit out back under the mesquite trees on the wobbly picnic table he was always on me to lay a fresh coat of paint on.

"Something fancy," he'd say. "Maybe a Moroccan red."

Mostly, though, we'd laugh, and try to forget about that night at the stadium and Roland and Danny. We tried to forget the years that were mostly gaps to him after Mom firefooted out and he went to drinking. We tried.

The quiet of the house wasn't like any kind of quiet before. The silence was damp and dreary and curled from the bottoms of my bare feet to the top of my head. I closed my eyes, drew in a deep breath just as I had after seeing Dad's body. Something was wrong. I gripped the couch cushions, my breath stuck somewhere in my windpipe. I couldn't get it back out. Breathe—just breathe. Things don't have to fall apart.

I heard the back door suck shut from the wind running through the open windows. I exhaled. Danny peeled off his jacket, not giving me so much as a glance while he flung it over Dad's garage-sale recliner. I started to make a sandwich while he shuffled his mass of hair, seeming overwhelmed at the spread. He scanned the lopsided table piled with platters of barbecue, enchiladas, rice and beans, and sandwich fixings of all kinds. There were deep bowls of potato salad, corn on the cob, fried okra, peas and three apple and cherry pies.

He slathered mayo on two thick slices of Texas toast. His big busted-up hands, fingernails trimmed with grease and dirt, trembled just enough for me to wonder why. He crammed thick leafy lettuce and wet red tomatoes, Ruffles and hunks of barbecue, smashing it all with one hard compression, leaving an ashy imprint of his hand.

Danny reached across the table for a sweaty can of Pepsi and knocked the mayo off. *CRASH!*

Shards of sticky glass scattered like pasty marbles. He popped back a couple of steps real nervous and frustrated like he'd done something just awful. For the first time, we looked right at each other. His eyes were like a long dim-lit hallway. They ran a chill up and down my spine two times over.

Danny manhandled the roll of paper towels, wadding them up into a big ball. After he wiped up the mess off the floor, he flung the towels on a paper plate and splotches of red were all over them. He held up his right hand, realizing without any shock or alarm that he'd cut himself real good.

"It's deep," I said, my eyes on my sandwich.

"I know." He stared at the gash.

The maroon blood dribbled down onto the plastic tablecloth.

I held out a hand towel. "It's clean."

He considered the offer. Then wrapped it around his palm real snug.

"Doctor's open 'til six," I said.

"It'll heal." He snapped up his sandwich. "You've gotten big. Bigger."

I huffed, half rolling my eyes.

"Taller," he said. "I could see that when you were sitting at the funeral."

"You didn't even look at me."

He stared down between his sandwich for some clue of what to say.

"You play anything?" he said, taking a gigantic chomp out of the sandwich. "Sports, I mean."

"No."

Danny waited for me to say something else or for my head to spin in a full three-hundred-and-sixty-degree circle.

"Well," he said, bobbing his head like a fishing cork over water.

He dug his uninjured hand in the Ruffles and plopped on the living room floor in front of the TV, clicking through the only three channels we got. Danny was exactly the same but bigger somehow. Not fat . . . just . . . fuller. But empty.

He twisted around as if he could feel me watching him. We stared at each other as he chewed. And chewed and chewed and—

"Anyone home?" said Uncle Jack, thumping on the screen door and coming in.

Danny finished off his sandwich in a hearty cheek-stuffing bite. I walked over and hugged Uncle Jack. Danny watched for a moment before leaning back toward the TV.

"I just wanted to stop back by," Uncle Jack said. "Make sure you two were doing all right."

"I'm ready to go," I said, heading for my bedroom. "I just need to come back and pack up the other stuff this weekend."

"Well, I thought maybe Danny and I could have a chat for a moment. Now that he's had some time to get settled."

Danny settled? His duffel bag was still in the bed of the truck.

"What do you say, Danny?" said Uncle Jack.

"What do I say?" asked Danny, his eyes on the TV.

"Talk, son. Outside."

Danny considered the proposition for a moment, then dusted the crumbs off his faded jeans, knocking them onto the carpet.

"What happened to your hand there?" Uncle Jack asked, with a concern I couldn't have mustered.

"Nothing," Danny said. "Just a scratch."

Uncle Jack looked at me and I shrugged. Wasn't my problem.

I stood at the screen door as the two of them headed far enough to be out of earshot. Danny kept his head down mostly or looked right past Uncle Jack altogether. At first, Uncle Jack looked over his shoulder, trying to figure out what Danny was looking at, before realizing it was nothing. Just space. Danny nodded, all the while beating his boot heel into the dirt along the driveway. A dense low-key burst of dusty smoke swam around his feet. Dad useta do the same thing when people talked to him.

The stronger and more ornery Danny got around Dad,

the more they'd go at each other like two rabid dogs in a five-by-five cage. And if Dad was on the whiskey he could be as ferocious as an onion sack of rattlesnakes in the summer heat.

Danny looked over at me and I backed up from the door. I didn't know whether to get my stuff together or what, so I started putting up the food. I slid the lids on the casserole dishes and had started rolling the corn on the cob in a sheet of foil when I thought about his jacket. I tipped my head around the living room curtains and saw the two of them were still talking. I walked over to the recliner and stuck my hand in the inside pocket. I found a half-melted Hershey's bar with loose peanuts and a stick of Wrigley's chewing gum stuck to it. I lifted the flap of his breast pocket with my other hand and pulled out a Greyhound ticket stub:

DEPARTURE: Madison, Wisconsin
ARRIVAL: Three Rivers, Texas

In capital letters, printed below that: ONE WAY. I heard the front gate close, and I stuffed the stub back in his pocket. Danny stepped in the screen door, slamming it behind him.

"What did he say?" I asked.

He snapped the cordless phone off the charger and headed for his old bedroom.

"I gotta make a phone call."

"Hey," I said, following him into the hall. "You don't have to be so mean to me, you know. I'm not a little kid anymore."

He stopped at the edge of his door. "I have never been mean to you."

He fumbled with the knob and disappeared into his bedroom. A wave of panic crashed over me. I flung the screen door open as Uncle Jack's car drove away. He waved to me, a sure sign I wasn't gonna be happy anytime soon.

3

LET THE EXCELLENCE IN YOU SHINE THROUGH

I stared dumbfounded at the cheesy laminated yellow sign with faded pink and purple flowers. It was firmly taped to the outside door of the high school guidance counselor's office. They called me out of world history with a note that said *Excused*. I hadn't asked to be excused from a quiz the day after Dad's funeral. I hadn't asked to be called out in front of the class full of juniors just waiting for some kind of stupid dramatic freak-out like Rosa Olivarez when her brother died in Iraq. I hadn't asked for anything, not even breakfast from my locker-room-smelling brother stumbling around in chewed-up navy warm-ups and a single white sock. I didn't eat.

I woke up that morning with my head up, not wanting any excuses of any kind. I just wanted to forget the whole last week. So the last thing I wanted was a pass to Mrs. Alvarado's office, which was clear away from the main part of school in a khaki-colored portable building. Everyone had to have seen me from their classroom windows walk all the way out there, which meant everyone would be saying by second period how I needed someone to talk to. Or that maybe this would be the thing that would finally make me crazy—crazy like my brother, and I just might burn the whole school down before fourth period.

I lightly knocked, hoping she might not hear over the rattling of the dripping window unit. Then I could say I went but no one answered. But behind the door a muffled, peppy "Come in" meant there was no way to wiggle out of it.

I stepped in, awkwardly standing as close to the door as I possibly could. Mrs. Alvarado was always real chatty with us kids but she never really had anything to say. We hadn't talked much since I aced the PSATs last year and was bumped up to honors and a couple of Saturday classes every other weekend at a junior college a county over. She mostly smiled with her plump face caked in makeup cracking in places. In fact, Mrs. Alvarado smiled a lot even though her husband left her and her two kids a year ago to be with a dental hygienist from San Antonio. She came to school every day and smiled. For some reason, that really scared me.

"Hey there, Michelle," she said, coming around her desk.

She wrapped her flabby arms around me and *squeezed*. "I am so sorry that you are having to go through this."

So was I. She smelled like burnt potpourri and cheap perfume.

"Sit down," she said. Her flowery dress snagged the edge of the desk. She kept smiling. "So, Michelle . . ."

She started talking about loss and love and something about the birth canal. My eyes tagged the tidy office lined with neat stacks of college catalogs and overflowing book-shelves of three-ring binders and paperback books with their pages on entrance exams and personal growth. The walls carefully mounted with laminated posters of kittens and puppies and a gazillion framed pictures of her kids in all kinds of costumes. They were smiling too. Everything in that office was smiling, even the tile on the floor. My stomach started to burn and toss and turn—

"With all that to say," she said, taking a moment to breathe, "I suppose I just want to ask, how are you?"

There was this new color coating her sage eyes as if opportunity had finally come to her. As if she had eagerly waited each day for trauma to unleash on us kids, so she'd have something to do besides track our academic careers or write letters of recommendation. Letters that rarely got anyone into anywhere but a community college and not for very long.

"Michelle?"

"I'm okay," I said, hoping to get out easy, but the pause put me at risk of further discussion, or worse yet another one of those gagging hugs.

She leaned on her elbows, pressing her folded-over fingers against her chin, nodding her head. It made my skin crawl to have anyone look at me that long behind wide-framed glasses. I stretched my mouth into a half—and I mean *very* halfhearted—smile and started nodding along with her. There wasn't any music. There wasn't anything, so why we were nodding I sure didn't know.

"It's ohh-kay to talk about what you're feeling," she said.

I had started my period in the middle of the night and all I was feeling was tired, fat, and crampy. I didn't need to share that with her. I rolled the toe of my shoe along the raised-up linoleum floor square. The snap-tap evolved into a messy cadence of tic, tic, tica-tica as I rocked back and forth in the chair.

"These are hard times, they sure are. It isn't easy losing a parent."

She wanted to say another parent, but guidance counselors quit talking about Mom after Danny flipped his lid. Seemed better not to add kindling to the fire, so to speak.

She reached in her side desk drawer; her fingers crawled along the edges of manila folders. "Are you feeling sad?" Her brow dipped down, her eyes more focused on the files. "Michelle?"

"My brother's back. I don't know for how long," I said.

It was the only thing I could think to say. From Mrs. Alvarado's expression, I quickly realized I might as well have blurted out, "The Holocaust Rules!" and saluted Hitler. Roland had been her shining star. Even if he was a wildcard off the field, not that anyone would ever say it, he was a

Mexican with an unbelievable talent. A talent unmatched by any other Mexican in the history of our town of mostly Mexicans. The way they rallied around him, it made sense he'd think he had the keys to the kingdom . . . a god on earth. Too bad he didn't know that gods could fall.

Just when I thought Mrs. Alvarado's scrunched-up prune-like face would hold steady, it stretched back out into a smile. She laid out a pamphlet entitled "Losing Someone You Love."

Her thick slick acrylic fingernails clawed it open to a drawing of a girl crying in a woman's arms. Beside that, a boy raised his eyes hopefully to a man with his arm around him. The blurb over all of them:

Grief Is Okay . . . You Are Okay.

Was she serious? I looked up at her blankly.

"Whatever you're feeling, it is ohh-kay. Do you understand?"

I had no idea what she was saying, but her smile made me figure I should, so I nodded.

"I want you to read this. It will help get you through."

I slid the pamphlet off her desk, tucked it in my back pocket, and got up to leave before the stupid smiling room closed in on me.

"You're an exceptionally bright young lady, Michelle," said Mrs. Alvarado. "You let me know if you're having any trouble. My door is always open."

That was a complete and total lie. It was always closed. Always.

I cut out of there and strained to take a deep breath. I hated my dad for dying and making me sit there for the last five minutes. I hated that she hated Danny as much as I did, only for different reasons, and she hadn't earned it by a mile. Mostly, I hated that I had the worst cramps probably ever and thought I might just hurl.

I walked the long way back to the main part of school. Just as I cut the corner toward the door to senior lockers, I saw Ricky Martinez strutting from the parking lot with his best friend, Johnny Lee Miller. Ricky's skater-cut hair hung loose in his face. He reached up to push it back, and the upside-down James Brown permanent-inked on the back of his hand moved across his cheek. I had managed to sit next to him every year in history since junior high. We didn't really ever talk, so it made a lot of sense that I was stumped when he said, "Hey, Mickey. Wait up."

I propped the door open with my foot. The cool air-conditioning ran up the cuff of my blue jeans and sent a quick shiver all over me. It was kind of an embarrassing thing to happen in front of guys like Ricky and Johnny Lee.

"Michelle," Johnny Lee said, standing closer than he had since elementary. "I'm real sorry . . ." And he paused, searching for whatever was rattling around in his head. "About your dad. Really."

Johnny Lee was kind of a mystery to most. He didn't talk much, dug fences with his father and always had a paperback in his pocket where a wallet or a can of snuff would've been. He and Ricky both played football, which immediately elevated any guy around school to godlike status, but the fact that Johnny Lee was as good, if not maybe better than Roland Gonzalez made him a potential king. His looks were gentle and I'd seen girls draped all over him but it didn't seem his thing. Weird.

But Ricky, he was the real mystery cloud as far as I was concerned. He was the only flunkie in the history of kindergarten who wasn't dumb by a mile and three quarters. He refused outright to cut and paste and take naps in the afternoon because he wanted to read comics and write poems. Plus, as the story goes because I was a year behind, he would come in late every day after recess because he sat in the sandbox staring up at the sky. And every day, the principal dragged him back to class while he kept saying, "I'm waiting. I'm waiting for it to fall."

I always thought that was the coolest. I took naps even when I wasn't supposed to.

"Thanks for the offer," Johnny Lee said to Ricky. "Catch you later." And a hand slap-shake, "See ya, Michelle," and he disappeared into the building.

"I gotta get some adventure in that guy, Mickey. You don't live forever." Ricky's grin melted away in a matter of seconds as he realized that was the worst kind of thing you could say to someone whose dad just died.

He stepped back from me, pressing his large hands with sports tape wrapped on his index fingers onto the stair railing.

"Sorry," he said, scratching the toe of his black Vans in a little pile of dirt on the step. "So . . . what are you doing out here?"

Like I was gonna tell him I'd just come back from the portable nuthouse. I felt in my back pocket, the one without the pamphlet, and held up the Excused slip.

"I was just coming back from running an errand for the office."

27

"You're a bad liar." He grinned. His hair half draped his flawless complexion. "We're in the same first-period class."

My stomach squirmed. How could I've been on his radar in first period with the gaggle of girly-girls always passing notes to him?

"What are you really doing out here?" he said.

I looked off to the side. What was I going to say to the best-looking guy in the class? That I was being pamphletized?

He tilted his head just low enough to catch my eye-line.

I reluctantly pulled the pamphlet out of my pocket and sort of thrust it at him. He bent it open, reading in a sort of melody, "Grief is okay; you are okay."

"Yeah, that's supposed to make me feel better or something."

He half laughed.

"Mrs. Alvarado?"

I nodded.

"Yeah, when my grandmother died freshman year she gave me something like this. It was . . . weird."

Yeah, I thought. Weird was definitely how it felt. Weird and lame. He handed it back to me.

"The hotline on the back is okay, though. I mean, not that I'm saying you'd need to call. It's just . . . anyway."

And he went back to scratching the toe of his shoe on the step. I stuck the pamphlet back in my jeans. Watched this toned, black-haired guy who I'd only thought about enough times not even to repeat to Christina stand in front of me.

"What were you and Johnny Lee up to?" I asked.

"Nothing. Tried to get him to ditch Hodges' class alto-gether to go into the city. But you know Johnny Lee."

"Not really," I said.

"Well, he's in a lot of your classes, right?"

"Right . . . ," I said as some stupid nervous smile loosened on my face.

What was wrong with me? Standing that close to him, which I guess five feet wasn't close, I could feel the heat throbbing on my cheeks, flushing my face radish red. He didn't say a word about it.

"So . . . I'm sorry about your father. I wanted to go to the funeral but that's all so . . . you know?"

In the huge awkward pause that followed, he didn't once smile. I liked that. We just stood there feeling the uncomfortable weight of uncomfortable, and that was comfortable. Kind of.

"Everyone in town liked him a lot," Ricky said, making minicircles with his shoe. "He fixed up my dirt bike a couple of weeks ago for almost nothing."

"I know, I worked on it," I said.

"Yeah?" He raised his head with a gleam of excitement in his eyes.

"Yeah, between my dad and my brother, I knew more about cylinders than I ever did Barbie dolls."

"That's really cool," he said. "Really. Most of the girls I know, well, you know."

"No."

He blew air out the side of his mouth.

We stood there swamped again in the strained silence that I'd never had with a guy before. 'Cause I'd never really had anything with a guy except a really bad kiss in sixth grade and have regretted it every moment since.

The wind wailed, kicked up and swirled small funnels of dirt with chip bags and cup lids in the parking lot. Some of the wind broke our way and as he moved closer to me, it caught our hair, tossing and pairing our strands to dance. Ricky's green eyes glowed against his soft brown skin. The deafening wind tunneled into my ears. Before I could catch my breath or think to look down at my busted-up sneakers it whooshed on, and he dropped back against the wall.

"So you must be feeling really bad," he said. "I mean, like I said, when my grandmother died I felt like . . . I don't know. Like something was, like, missing but not in a dumb way. Like . . . just gone."

I must have felt bad. I mean, that was what people felt, didn't they? He did. He did and he only knew my dad for fixing up his dirt bike.

"It's a good thing your brother's sticking around."

"No one's said anything like that," I snapped.

"Oh . . . I just thought. I mean, I heard he was back. I just . . . don't you want him around? I remember the two of you always together."

Big awkward pause.

"I have to go back to class," I said, swinging the door wide open. "You know, we're having a quiz. You might want to stay at least for that."

He sigh-smiled. "I'm not a dumb jock, you know."

"There's a lot of adventure in there," I said, nodding inside. "Besides, you don't live forever, right?"

"Right," he said, reaching his hand over my head, holding the door open. "Right."

4

The number two school bus kicked up a swirling gust of dirt and hot air as it flew by Christina and me.

"Okay, this walking thing is stupid, especially in May. Maybe October but never May," she said, fanning her melting makeup.

She'd complain if it were October too. She hated to walk.

"I'm gonna kill Hector if I find out he went to see that girl in the Valley instead of picking us up. Loose-legged bimbo."

"Doesn't he want to marry her?"

"He better not," she said.

Ninety-four degrees flashed on the First National State

Bank sign. I fanned my T-shirt, trying to forget my aching feet. It was a good two and a half miles from the high school to my house. A stretch of weathered buildings home to the H-E-B Grocery, Glass Pharmacy, a couple of card-table restaurants and two florist shops that survived mostly on funerals and football season. Everything else along the strip people called the "two-light main street" was mostly boarded up with cheap plywood spray-painted in maroon and white: THREE RIVERS STATE CHAMPS or MIGHTY PIRATES STEAL DISTRICT!

Six years since the state victory, no one thought to paint over it. The town needed football like most people needed water. Thanks to Johnny Lee and Ricky we made it to Regional Semifinals last year before a hard hit laid Johnny Lee out in the third quarter. Would they've won if he'd kept playing? Maybe. Didn't really matter 'cause he did get hit and that was just how it went with luck in our town.

Past the Aycock Gas and Go, a little ways closer to the Catholic church, was Dad's garage. Well, what useta be his. He lost it to the bank a couple years into Mom leaving. Albert had started working there back when he was in high school and worked out some deal to buy it. So, Andy's Autos and Repair became Trevino's Autos and Repair in a few strokes of paint. When Dad dried out, Albert gave him a job as co–head mechanic and, from what Uncle Jack said, a siz-able percentage of the business. Maybe that was what drug Danny's dead bones back to town. I hadn't even thought about money until right then. I just figured on Uncle Jack getting me through.

Christina and I waved to Albert, who stood under a 1978 cinnamon Olds. He half grinned with the side of his mouth struggling to stay up.

"This is a mess," Albert said, wiping his hands with a faded red grease rag. "Feel free to help me with it."

"Maybe this weekend. Gotta study tonight," I said.

"Hey, Mickey, wait."

Albert ducked in the office and came out carrying a plate covered in foil.

"Priscilla wanted me to take this over to the house later. She just keeps baking and baking. I hope she has those babies soon or I'll be too fat to pick them up."

"Thanks," I said, heading off with Christina.

"Mickey."

"Yeah?"

"Tell your brother I said hi. To come by if he wants. Okay?"

I nodded and crossed the street with Christina. Soon as our feet hit the broken sidewalk wrapped around the church, she did that Catholic cross/kiss the necklace thing.

"Does that make you feel better?" I asked. "I mean, all that crossing stuff."

"No." She laughed. "Well, maybe kinda, but it definitely makes my mother feel better. I don't know how many candles she's lit wishing I was like the rest of the family. The fact that I hold on to our religion is like some kind of light at the end of the tunnel that I'll get dumb and have lots of babies like her and my aunts. She was on me last night saying, 'You'll never get a man the way you're behaving. Always reading and smart-talking.' I told her maybe I don't want a man or if I do, I don't wanna be like her and marry the first *cabron* with a coolio car and a greasy smile."

"What'd she say?"

"She slapped me," Christina said, her whole face twisted up angry. "Right there in the restaurant at the register."

"Are you serious?"

"She said how dare I disrespect her. Whatever. It's like with you. When she picked me up from your house yesterday, she told me, 'You're lucky you didn't have to grow up like that girl. What a horrible shame.' Like she don't even see you. She just sees the messed-up stuff around you. I think it's better that your mom split than drag you down all the time. Sometimes I wish I was that lucky."

I threw my arm over her shoulders. A strange gesture between girls our age unless you were on the cheerleading squad or huddled up before a basketball game. This wasn't a town of touchy people, but there I was with my arm over her shoulders because I hated to see her cry.

"I'm fine," she said. "Besides, you're the one who should be venting. And I know you've been holding something in. You weren't even paying attention at lunch when I told you about my cousin getting trapped in the airport bathroom."

"Something . . . weird happened today."

"Okay, I'm ready. Tell me," she said, already out from under my arm and into Christina high alert.

"You know Ricky Martinez . . . he came up and *talked* to me when I was coming back from Mrs. Alvarado's office."

"No freaking way!" Her mouth was open wide enough to

net a few dozen flies. "I knew you looked different in second period. You said it was cramps."

"That wasn't a lie. And it wasn't a big thing, so don't start," I said.

"You've only had your eyeballs flypapered to his Trapper Keeper since forever and ten damn years. Ricky 'The Ghost' Martinez. He's only the best catch in the school and totally unattached."

"You were saying he was stupid just yesterday."

"You don't have to be as smart as the two of us to be a catch. And maybe I was being a little—"

"Little . . . ?"

"Okay, he's totally hot and I had a crush on him when I first moved here—"

"Shut up—"

"But thank Jesus, I have vowed no boys, no babies, no boys."

I wished that had been the only reason.

"Besides, I knew you had that *thing* for him," she said.

I could see the piñatas bursting in her head. Scattering all kinds of sweet images because it went right to her grin.

"It wasn't like a hookup," I said. "So you can settle your gossip gums down. We just talked."

"Right . . . ," she said, breaking into song. "Ricky and Mickey sittin' in a tree. K-I-S-S-I-N-G."

"How are you two points smarter than me?"

"First comes love. Then comes—oh my God. You are not going to marry this guy. No way. You've got college."

"Shut up. I knew I shouldn't have told you."

We turned the corner to my house with her spouting off a lecture about how it was awesome to get to know him but that my future came first. At least she didn't mention the birth canal.

We stopped at the edge of my overgrown front yard sprinkled in bluebonnets and daisies.

"You know, you can sleep over at my place," she said. "I could sneak you in."

"It's cool." I huffed out a frustrated sigh and made for the house. "You working at the restaurant tonight?"

"Only for a couple of hours," she said. "I can get out of it."

I swung open the rusty gate. "No you can't. I'll see you tomorrow. Meet you at the store around seven-thirty?"

"Okay. Oh and hey," she shouted. "Bring the truck. No more of this walking, Gringa."

I dragged up the porch steps and let the screen door slam shut behind me. The mixed smell of barbecue sauce and apples streamed from the kitchen into the living room. A sure sign he wasn't gone and wasn't gonna be, at least before dinner.

I dumped my backpack on the couch, noticing a letter addressed to Danny poking out from beneath a pile of circulars and bills. I tilted my head to read the return address written in strong, legible handwriting:

K. S. Smith
888 CR A
Iola, WI 54945

The toilet flushed and Danny stepped out of the bathroom, shaking his hands dry, wiping them on his jeans.

"You're here?" he said.

"Yeah?"

He slipped the letter into his back pocket as if I hadn't noticed it.

"Thought it might be another half hour or so."

I was still holding the plate Albert had given me.

"Here, Priscilla sent it. Albert said to come by if you want."

"The garage?"

I nodded, completely annoyed that I had to say anything to him. He didn't deserve one single word.

He peeked under the foil and snapped a cookie in half.

"Oatmeal raisin," he said, offering me one.

I shook my head, kicking the side of the couch with my sneaker.

He kept looking at me as he chewed and chewed and chewed that half a cookie. What the hell was he looking for?

"They must let you out earlier now." He swallowed the last of what had been in his mouth. Rooting around the back of his teeth with his index finger to unwedge some morsel. "The school. They let you out earlier."

I stood there, antsy and wanting to cut around him and go to my room, when I noticed the smell.

"Are you burning something on purpose?" I said.

"The potatoes . . ." He rushed for the kitchen. "You hungry? I got some good cooking in here."

I trailed behind him where he'd set the kitchen table with a repeat/reheat of yesterday's layout for the most part.

"It's a little early for dinner, isn't it?" I said, standing in the doorway.

"Well, I was hungry, and I wasn't sure when you eat, so I just figured . . ." He manhandled a skillet of brown gravy, spattering all over the stove. "Sit."

I pulled out a chair, the one closest to the door, still thinking about that letter from Wisconsin. Who would write to Danny? What would they say?

"You planning on getting a lot of mail here?" I asked.

"Nope."

My afternoon was already getting better with the prospects of him cutting loose again. No mail, no Danny. No Danny, no more trying to be polite.

"Supper's ready," he said, sliding out a slab of sickly ribs from the oven.

Suddenly the oven seemed an endless pit as he pulled out a foil of meat loaf, a casserole dish of yams, dinner rolls and half an apple pie.

Danny busied back and forth, cramming the table dish-to-dish, leaving our own plates hanging from the edges. He heaped a milky glob of mashed potatoes with little scorched flecks onto my plate.

"It's still good," he said. "Just pick around it."

He plopped uncomfortably into his chair, shifting around like Goldilocks until he found a spot that was just right, or right enough to get through supper.

"Learn anything in school?" he asked, stabbing a rib with his fork and sliding it off onto my plate.

"Not really," I said, wondering if he'd start cutting up my meat next.

"Jack says you're in a special program. That you're

graduating a year early in a few weeks. That's a real accomplishment, Mickey."

"Michelle," I corrected, poking at my food like a three-year-old.

"Michelle," he said. "Especially around here."

"Yeah, I guess."

His eyes bounced from my plate to me, signaling it was time to eat. I wanted to dig a hole in the backyard and bury my meal.

"They called me into Mrs. Alvarado's office today," I said.

There was a long pause before he asked, "Mrs. Alvarado?"

I nodded.

"She says it's normal if I'm feeling bad."

"She does, huh?"

He squeezed the ketchup bottle 'til it splattered red in one big gush.

"You feeling bad?" I asked.

His fingers wiped around the edge of the bottle before snapping it shut.

"Bad." He considered the word like it had been introduced to him for the first time. "Aren't you gonna eat?"

I watched him thrust his fork down into a mix of potatoes and peas with a hunk of groggy meat loaf. Who did he think he was, coming into Dad's house and not even knowing what the word *bad* meant? He knew. I got up from the table and headed for my room.

"I can make something else," he called after me.

"I'm not hungry."

He got up and followed me into the living room.

"You wanna go for a ride after dinner?" he asked.

"I got homework."

"It'll be fun. We could go out on The Stick. You ever go out there?"

"No, Danny, I don't. Okay?" I said, standing at the door of my bedroom. "And I don't eat food that sat out all night and day—"

"It was in the fridge—"

"I'm not a little kid anymore where you can just shove something under me and say 'eat.' "

We stood there with the silence and smell of burnt leftovers between us.

"I could fix you something else," he said.

"Just don't do anything. Okay?" I shut my bedroom door.

I locked the knob, leaned up against the wall, and my stomach squalled. I pulled out a half-eaten pack of peanut butter crackers I got from the vending machine at school. My hands shook and any other time I would have called out to Dad, "I gotta eat now."

And he'd say . . . and right then my throat got tight. Felt like angry hands were choking the life right out of me. Danny knocked on the door. A sloppy boy's knock.

"Mickey, Michelle. Can I come in?"

"I got homework," I said, feeling light-headed.

"Your book bag is out here on the couch."

"Go away, Danny."

I tried to get the cracker down. It wouldn't go. It was like my throat swelled and closed all the way up. Leaving a pin-prick of a hole for air to squirm through.

I dropped back on my bed and listened to the neighbor's wind chimes softly clang together. Sounded like the triangle I played at the Christmas concert freshman year—before I quit band. Before I realized I had to stop trying to please a brother who was never coming back.

"Mickey—Michelle, I'm gonna respect you and not come in but . . ."

There was a long pause. My throat ached and pulsated.

"I think," he said, "I think we should get outta here and talk. I think that would be good."

I could almost feel him breathing against the door. Exhaling deep dark breaths laced in rings of smoke and sparks of crimson-orange glow. I imagined opening the door after he'd gone to bed, or maybe flat out vanished, and there would be a charcoal imprint right where he'd been breathing.

"I'm still your brother."

"Fine! I'll go." My voice cracked on the last part. "Please, just leave me alone for a while."

He waited a moment, whatever a moment is, and then his footsteps got farther and farther away. The constriction in my throat lessened.

I fished in my nightstand drawer, sifting through a couple of packs of gum and papers. Stuck between my essay on *Of Mice and Men* and the free calendar from the Three Rivers Feed Co-op was the picture Uncle Jack took of Danny grad-uation night. Danny had his back to the camera, his head turned just enough to show the haunting deadness in his eyes. I wished they could've put that photo in the paper after the stadium burnt down instead of his class picture, because none of us knew that class-picture guy anymore. Not even him, I figured.

5

Wasn't any kind of streetlight out on The Stick. Not a splash except from the full moon occasionally peeking out from a breath of lazy clouds, outlining our faces and leaving the fields and telephone poles dim half-shapes.

Danny dropped the tailgate of the truck for the two of us to sit on. The only reason I even went out to that little scraggle of a road we always called The Stick was because I was hoping a little pretend bonding time might send him on his way sooner. He stretched across the back of the pickup and slid over a cooler with a tray of ice cubes dumped over a couple cans of soda. He cracked an RC and we sat there with our legs dangling in the darkness.

An evening breeze sent the cornstalks to talking and

echoed feelings I'd locked up a long time ago. Growing up, The Stick was our refuge. Mom's moods and Dad's drinking, it all faded the second our shoes stepped out on that narrow dirt road snaking between two cornfields. Compared to PlayStation, high-speed Internet or digital cable, being out on a slink of unpaved road might've seemed pretty boring. For the both of us, right up until the accident, it was a magical place. Just like reading *The Outsiders,* out there we belonged. You could be an astronaut or an explorer. A daredevil or a groupie. There was no limit to the transformations of the vast openness. When the crops grew in the spring, taking full stance by summer, we'd create bigger and better ideas. Our version of New York City or Las Vegas . . . Paris or the northern lights. It was all about imagination . . . about believing.

When we weren't making up some place or tucked beneath the stalks rereading *The Outsiders,* we were sky-watching. Danny was all about the sunsets and sunrises, which made sense from that book. But me, I liked the storms. Storms could be spotted from any direction for miles on The Stick. We'd sit out there ooohing and ahhhing as the sky would swell all up and blacken like a really painful bruise. Once during Danny's sophomore year, we saw a twister peek out some fifteen or so miles away. We ran something crazy and I was shaking so hard thinking we might get sucked right up into the sky and dunked into the Gulf of Mexico. Our sneakers hit the porch just as the hail hammered down. Danny squeezed my hand and said so excited, "Make a wish. It doesn't matter what falls. You can still make a wish."

I must've made hundreds of wishes between the hail and

the rain. It was the most fun I ever had in a storm, and I was never afraid of one since.

And there we were eight-some-odd years later, sitting on the back of Dad's truck and me barely standing the sound of Danny's breathing.

"I know about this arrangement you have with Jack," said Danny. "He told me yesterday. You want something like that? To live with him again?"

I shrugged.

"Makes the most sense," I said, looking up at the moon.

Danny cleared his throat. "I haven't stayed much in one place until recent. I mean, I don't know. I've got a lot happening around me. . . . I ain't never really settled right with this town." He finished his RC in a big gulp, crushed the can and chucked it in the truck bed. "Probably never will."

He leaned forward so he could dig his heel into the dirt.

"Well. Say something, Michelle. I figured you'd have something to say."

"What? You don't owe me anything. So don't worry about the big brother stuff, okay? It won't take me a night to pack my things and go back over to Uncle Jack's."

"Why'd you move back in with Dad? Last I heard you were with Jack."

"Yeah, when was that? Six years ago?"

Danny pounded his boot heel harder.

"I kept in touch after a while," he said. "Called Jack a couple of times. Now, don't go spinning your plugs. It was a couple of sentences, and he never knew where I was up until the last year."

Uncle Jack knew. All that time, he knew if Danny was

dead or alive. He didn't say a word to me. For a second, I didn't know who to be more pissed at. But it was a fast second because Danny was the one beside me.

"Whatever," I said. "Let's just go."

"I just don't get it, Michelle. After everything that man did to us growing up—"

"To you. To you, Danny. People can change. Whatever went on between you and Dad, it had nothing to do with me."

"What are you saying? The guy was a drunk."

I hopped off the tailgate.

"He sure didn't mind knocking the hell out of me," said Danny. "Who do you think made sure he never laid a hand on you?"

"I'm not kidding. I wanna go."

"I'm trying to talk to you. I want to understand."

"You always wanted to make him out to be the bad guy, Danny. You know what, though? He didn't leave. He stuck it out. He went to meetings. He *talked* things through."

Danny nodded. "I talked to Jack today. About Dad's accident."

"Shut up. You shut up."

"There was alcohol in his blood, Michelle."

"He wasn't drunk."

"Does it matter how much alcohol?" he asked. "He was a drunk almost our whole lives."

I just wanted to hit him. So I did. Pushed him right off the tailgate.

"Michelle Ann—"

"You shut up and do whatever you want, Danny. But

don't you go passing judgment on me or Dad, 'cause you ain't got the right. You weren't here. Not for this one."

Every part of me knew digging into my brother like that was belly-up low, but I wasn't going to have him mark me as some dumb kid who couldn't stand up for herself.

I cut out of there, warm tears bubbling all over my cheeks. Forget him and forget Dad. Forget Mom and forget the stupid guidance counselor and her crappy pamphlets.

Just forget it!

That was when he came jogging up behind me.

"Slow down," he said, hooking my elbow. "Hey. Look, I'm sorry—I'm sorry he died."

"No you ain't."

"You're right. I ain't. But I'm sorry that you feel bad. And yeah, it's okay to feel bad as long as that's what you're really feeling and you're not feeling how you *think* you should feel."

I looked at him totally lost.

"Erase that." Danny said. "Just . . . look. Stand still."

He couldn't fetch up something to say, so he started pacing, kicking up waves of dust with his boot.

"Okay, are you listening?" he said.

I heaved a deep breath.

"I think I should stay. For a while."

"No. No way, Danny. If it's about a will or getting money outta the garage, Uncle Jack will fix it up for you."

"How low do you think I am? It's me, Mickey."

I glared at him. "Don't call me that."

I took off, walking even faster than before. Then I ran as

hard as I could with nothing but dim blue glow filling out the slinking dirt road.

"I ain't gonna chase you," he shouted. "I ain't."

He had driven us miles from anything paved or lit, but I knew the way. My heart roared in my chest, pounding like ten angry gorillas. My calves cramped up not after too long, but I kept running. My breath seared the back of my throat. When I got home, Dad would be there. He would have to be there so he could tell me one of his new lame jokes that he recalled in fragments. He would tease me about some boy he thought might be crushing on me and tell me I needed to give them boys a break because they need one every now and then. He'd be there to tell me it was going to be all right. It was finally going to be okay, even without Danny or Mom. We'd make it all right because we stuck. We stuck things through.

From behind, the low beams of the truck crawled up, making a lanky loose ten-foot shadow in front of me. I ran for as long as I could. Then I slumped forward with my hands resting on my shaky knees, struggling to catch my breath. The engine hiccuped. I squinted back at the truck cab. A dark shadow with the glowing end of a cigarette was all I could make out. Who was I kidding? It was a long walk home, and I was out of shape.

I climbed in the back of the truck and settled up against the toolbox, down low so he couldn't see me. He dropped the gear into drive and inched forward a few feet before jamming on the brakes. Next thing I knew, he slammed his door, hopped the tailgate and stood right there in the bed of the truck.

"I ain't doin' this 'cause you're pouting," Danny said.

"I'm not pouting," I said, slowly biting each word.

"Yeah, well." He looked at me as long as he could stand it before shouting, "Uhhh!"

Then he jumped up and down, shaking the whole truck. I crouched so far back I couldn't get any more up on the tool-box. He finally collapsed against the tire well. After catching his calm, he could see he'd scared me and got frustrated and nervous like when he broke that mayonnaise jar.

"I don't know a lot about being right," he said. "Can't we just try? Jack thinks it's a good idea."

"We'll see 'bout that," I said under my breath.

"Yeah, guess so."

There was no way my loony brother was going to have me believe Uncle Jack didn't want me. No way to the moon and back.

"Will you get in the cab?" he said, hopping off the truck bed. "It ain't safe back here. Come on."

Safe? What did my fire-footed brother know about safe?

"Please," he said.

I stood and stepped over the tailgate, hopping down.

"That ain't a snake, is it?" Danny asked.

I jumped back up on the truck bumper.

He grinned. He'd actually made a joke. It was an honest-to-God smile even if it faded into something lost really quickly.

As we drove back, I kept my eyes out the window. The moon and the big old Texas stars. There was a time I would've made a half a dozen wishes. It only occurred to me to make one, and so far, it was feeling like that wouldn't come true anytime soon.

"Hey," I said to Christina as I cut the corner of the magazine aisle at H-E-B Grocery. "What's in Wisconsin?"

Christina dutifully flipped through the current issue of *Tigerbeat*. She did that sort of thing so people wouldn't think she was so weird for reading the dictionary in three languages paperback for fun.

"You're late," she said, smacking her bubble gum.

"Long night. You get the Snapple?" I asked.

Still reading the magazine, Christina lifted her purse with a plastic bag peeking out the top.

"There's breakfast taquitos in there. Bean and *queso*. Totally high in protein."

I popped the Snapple lid open. "I already ate."

"You're lying," she said, not lifting her eyes from the flavor-of-the-month quiz. "You're lying to your best friend in the whole world. If you were Catholic, you'd go to hell. According to my mother and Father Jesus, anyway."

"I thought that was for premarital sex."

"We go to hell for a lot of things."

"Fine," I said. "I didn't eat and *don't* start with the lecture. I'll get something at school. So, do you know anything about Wisconsin?"

"Let's see." Her eyes squinted, peeling through her infinite mental Rolodex. "*That '70s Show, Happy Days, Laverne and Shirley.* And you know how crazy Texans are about football? Up there, they're totally loco. My cousin Adam whose brother moved up there to get away from his crazy ex-wife— you know, the one that smells like vinegar and onions and hits on high school boys—well, Adam's brother said those *gringos* are all kinds of crazy about football. Statewide green day for the Packers games. Oh, and Wisconsin has the only freshwater surfing championship in the world. Six- to ten- foot crests."

Christina was the encyclopedia of what seemed like useless information. She'd see a page once and remember nearly everything on it. It scared the hell out of her parents, who could barely read or write English. After she read *The Origin of the Species* in second grade, she decided to enlighten the kids at her old school during recess. She told them they all came from monkeys and then they told their parents, and their parents called her parents and before long she spent several shameful months with some whack-job headshrinker affiliated with the Catholic Church with a degree in stupid. He

51

convinced her parents that she had gotten "cured" and none of them would suffer eternal damnation for her infraction.

She still thinks we come from monkeys, sort of.

"Oh, and cheese," she said.

With a mouthful of Snapple, I repeated, "Cheese?"

She tucked a copy of *Newsweek* inside the *Tigerbeat*. "Yeah. It's the dairy state. Cows, churns, barns." She blew this swishy purple-pink bubble that almost covered her whole face. *POP!* "Well, that's Wisconsin. Cheese." Her eyes perked up at a headline in the business section. "You thinking about applying to the University of Wisconsin?"

"No, I'd just never noticed it on the map before and there it was."

Christina knew I was totally lying again but best friends let little things slide after a while. She shelved the magazines, and we headed out of the store. Soon as the mechanical glass doors slid sideways, a wave of sticky heat crashed into us.

"I am so glad we're not walking today," she said.

"Well . . . I couldn't exactly get the keys. . . . I'm gonna make it up to you, Christina."

Christina stopped walking and glared at me.

"I am," I said.

She started across the parking lot. "I snuck you taquitos, Gringa. Taquitos made by the ancestors of Mexicans who gave up this very land and now live here as visitors, not that I'm preaching even though we somehow have to watch *your* John Wayne in *The Alamo* every freaking year at school."

She shook her head, saddling her purse higher on her shoulder.

"Walk. No one in Texas walks, Mickey. I would've asked Hector to get up and drive us."

"Did I mention you're my best friend in the whole world?"

"Did I mention I'm sweating like a freaking pig? You *so* owe me."

"I know, I know. Come on."

We were about half a mile from the high school when Ricky's 1992 Ford Taurus coughed up next to me and Christina. The car was held together by duct tape and maybe bubble gum from the looks of it. Every bit of it vibrated, rattled like two rolls of loose coins in a tin can. Ricky shot out the driver's window *Dukes of Hazzard* style.

"Need a lift? I'm actually gonna try the whole 'making it to first period on time' today," he said.

"No, we're cool," I said.

"We are?" Christina barked.

"We can make room," said Johnny Lee in the passenger seat. "Really."

I leaned into Christina. "Since when do you want to ride with the jock squad?"

She raised her eyebrow, a clear indication that either we got in or I'd hear about it for the rest of the school year.

I sighed as Johnny Lee got out and popped the bucket seat up. Christina squeezed, and I mean squeezed, in the back filled with sports gear, thirty-two-ounce Coke bottles, *Auto Traders*, *PennySaver* ads with cleat marks, and piles of books.

"Sorry about that," Johnny Lee said to Christina. "Guess we need to clean the car more than once a year."

53

"There's an idea," Christina said, her foot caught on the back of the seat. "Wait, okay."

Johnny Lee crawled into the back with her.

"Well, what do you say?" said Ricky, still perched in the window. "I'm pretty sure it's getting close to tardy time."

He dropped into the driver's seat and before I got a foot in, the engine died. Christina heaved a jumbo sigh, picked up a *PennySaver* and started fanning.

"Don't worry," Ricky said. "For real. It does that when it idles too long."

Ricky turned over the ignition, pumping the accelerator in rapid taps.

"You're flooding it," I said, standing in the doorway hoping for a breeze.

"Nope. Just the right amount of . . ." and the car rattled back to life again. "See?"

"Andale, Gringa," said Christina. "We got, like, five minutes and that's if the saints are listening."

Ricky laughed as I tried to find a place for my feet on his floorboard littered with burger wrappers and paperback classics from the college reading list posted in the school library under the lunch menu.

"Johnny Lee and me kind of live in this car. We're gonna strut it up over the summer. Detail it." He tilted his head to the backseat. "Hey, Johnny Lee, toss up that car book we got in the city."

I could hear Johnny Lee digging around, crushing papers and clanging plastic bottles. He passed this generic kind of *How to Fix Your Car for Dummies* to Ricky, who dropped it into my lap.

"We got a couple of other ones. I want this car to purr senior year."

"Isn't it already purring?" Christina said sarcastically.

I glared over my shoulder at her. She was the last one who should be giving Ricky a hard time. It was her brilliant idea to take the ride.

Ricky slid a burnt mix into the CD player, the only upgrade to the car, and the dashboard rumbled to the beat of Tejano rap.

"Johnny Lee does a lot of the reading—not that I can't read. I'm more hands-on, I guess. You know?"

And somehow when his eyes met mine I felt my tongue go empty, so I just nodded back.

Ricky adjusted the rearview mirror.

"You got enough air back there?" he asked Christina.

"Not really," she answered.

"Have to crack the window."

A few seconds later, a horrible screeching came from the backseat and Johnny Lee was stretched over Christina jamming the window down with both hands. She was pushed so far back in the seat you would've thought he had the worst BO ever.

We hit a pothole and Johnny Lee lost his balance a little and bumped her and I could see her descend into freak-out. And he saw it too probably because he peeled back something fast, saying, "I'm sorry. Really, sorry," putting as much distance between them as he could without being on the roof.

I gave her the "you okay?" look but it didn't matter 'cause she wasn't okay. Guys made her nervous and for good reason. One of her dad's friend's, an all-around upstanding man, made more than a pass at her in junior high and when she told her parents they grounded her for months. Made her even apologize to the creep. And the worst part, she didn't even tell them how far the pervert went.

As we drove past the stadium rebuilt in concrete, my eyes stayed with the fluttering maroon and white ribbons flowing from the chain-link fence. A banner two people long pinned to it read: SENIOR PRIDE, SENIOR STRIDE! STATE TRACK MEET 2003!

"How come you don't run track?" I asked Ricky. "I mean, you're fast."

"You come to the games?"

"Ah, no. Everybody just knows you're fast, that's all. I mean, why else would they call you The Ghost?"

"That's a good question, huh?" he said.

And there my face started to burn again. I rolled the window down all the way, hoping to fan it off.

"Too much like a hamster in a cage," Ricky said. "No matter how much you run, you end up in exactly the same spot. Kind of stupid, don't you think?"

I caught Christina grinning in the rearview mirror. He wasn't a dumb jock, that was for sure. Not by a mile. Not by a mile and three-quarters even if he *had* flunked kindergarten.

"So my little cousin Teresa," Ricky said. "She's a freshman, she was over at the house last night. She says That Kid is okay."

"What kid?"

"That Kid, that cut in front of your dad with his dirt bike," Ricky said. "She's always hanging around with him. . . ."

I hadn't even thought about it really, Dad's accident. There were so many other things to get done. The sheriff had told me the details, but I'd muted them until right then. Right then, the roar of a dirt bike motor swelled in my ears—Dad swerved—he wasn't wearing a seat belt. He just went through—my skin was hot. I started counting in my head.

One, two, three four five six seveneightninteneleven . . .

"He just broke his arm," Ricky said, steering into the school parking lot.

Nineteen twenty twenty-one—Dad's neck—twenty-two . . .

"Tough thing to live with." The brakes squealed to a stop. "Anyway, he's supposed to come back next week. I thought you might've wanted to know."

Twenty-six twenty-seven twenty-eight twenty-nine . . .

"Mickey," Christina said softly.

"Huh?" I answered.

I'd heard every last word Ricky said and still mangled it together with, with . . . I don't know. It didn't matter because right then I looked up and saw the last bunch of kids sprint toward the school hoping to dodge a tardy.

"Thanks for the ride," I told Ricky, popping the door handle.

I released the seat and Johnny Lee crawled out. He held out his hand, fingernails lined in dirt, for Christina, but she kicked her own way out. Soda bottles and loose-leaf paper scattered onto the gravel lot. Christina chunked them back onto the floorboard but a few sheets caught a drifter wind and sailed off the gravel, somersaulting in the air. It was really kind of beautiful.

"You cool?" Christina asked as we headed for the breezeway.

I nodded, mainly because I didn't know if saying no made any more sense.

I picked up the pace, and she matched it. We split up at junior lockers, and I cleared the door to first period without a second to spare. Ricky was, of course, tardy.

On and off through first-period history, Ricky twisted around in his seat trying to get my attention. When the bell rang, I was the first to slip out of there, hoping to dodge anymore anything. But halfway to my locker, Ricky stepped in front of me.

"I'm sorry," he said with everyone moving around us. "I'm not sure what I'm sorry for but I am." He sucked in a deep breath. "I just thought you should know and I . . ." He ran his hand through his hair, tucking it behind his ear. "Do you wanna just, I don't know, talk sometime?"

"Why?"

He seemed wounded by the question.

"I, um." He nervously half laughed. "I don't know, I . . . Dumb, huh?"

"No, not dumb, I, I just can't . . . talk right now."

He nodded.

"Cool. Okay."

The minute I pivoted and walked toward my locker, I started screaming in my head how stupid that was. How stupid to not just have made up some feeling about my dad or my brother. How stupid not to be like every other girl tripping all over themselves for five seconds at the picnic tables outside the cafeteria with Ricky.

But the truth was, I didn't want to talk to anyone about anything to do with my family. Especially to the greatest guy in the entire school. Because if I said what I really felt, he would never talk to me again. No one would.

Christina had her nose in T. S. Eliot's *The Waste Land* when I dragged into second-period honors English.

"I can't believe I totally spaced," she said.

"What?"

"The test, Gringa. You forgot too? Quick, fake a headache."

"Right," I said, sliding into the desk beside hers.

Christina ripped through the pages as the bell rang. The last few stragglers shuffled to their desks. I looked to my left, a few rows over, and saw Johnny Lee with his eyes buried in a book of poetry by Carl Sandburg. He'd managed to study. Between probably working out in the weight room after school, helping Ricky with that car, and who knows, maybe even digging. And there he was reading a book that wasn't even on the syllabus, and I'd forgotten to read the one that was. Forgotten because of pamphlets and cramps, and of course, my loser brother. Thank God it was Friday.

Mrs. Briscoe immediately handed out the test while reciting the teacher's credo of eyes on your own paper, you have *X* number of minutes to finish. Et cetera, et cetera. Hand to hand, the wave of stapled pages descended back. The last thing I had on my mind was a test on *The Waste Land*, but there the fuzzy smudged purple-blue letters of true and false, multiple choice and essay looked up at me.

At what point did we ever really stop taking tests? I mean the real ones, the life tests. I thought Dad had, but in just one second, bam! Test over.

Mrs. Briscoe called my name from behind her desk. When I steadied out of the noise in my head, I started to feel really . . . sick. I reached for Christina's arm, but I don't think I ever touched it.

It was weird what cluttered my head with the honors English class huddled above me. I didn't think about anything big like the meaning of life or if I'd get kissed before graduation and like it. Everything got wiped away, funneled into this overwhelming sensation of falling—only I was already on the floor.

My skin felt hot. I saw Christina's face. Her lips mouthed it was going to be okay. I saw Mrs. Briscoe and just before I don't remember the next, my eye caught the edge of a guy's letterman jacket. I could've sworn it said Class of '98 along the sleeve. I could've sworn I smelled smoke. I tried to say something. I tried to move.

I tried to help him.

He was burning.

I woke up with Uncle Jack sitting at my side. I rose up quick but my head and the room went light and spun.

"Settle back. Breathe."

I eased back and heard the crinkle of a paper pillowcase.

"Where am I?" I asked.

"You're at the nurse's office," said Uncle Jack.

Uggh . . . the school nurse was the worst place to be taken. It was between the elementary and the junior high about two miles from the high school. Most of the action came from the tiny tykes, and the stockpile of chewable children's Tylenol and lollipops didn't do much for hypoglycemia. The room looked just like it had when I went there as a kid with my sour stomachs or fake headaches.

Big-lettered posters with pictures hung on the sterile walls. Happy little turtles and bears, trees and smiling stars and a dog running alongside a young boy with schoolbooks tucked beneath his arm. Everything in the room was geared toward being calm, being soothed, being young enough not to know what comes next. What comes after cute little animals and a fun day with Spot. When the letters got smaller and the words usually had a double and darker meaning. When you realized that everything can do more than sting. It can burn and sear and make you want to just curl up in a corner and turn off the light and wish you were running in that laminated world with that dumb smiling dog.

"You had yourself a spell," said Nurse Ample, standing in the doorway. "You about scared the good life out of your classmates."

She walked over and felt my forehead. Nurse Ample wasn't a local. She was from up north, way north near Canada which, given where we were, she might as well have been from the moon.

Nurse Ample leaned over me and beamed a penlight in my eyes, prying each one open real wide. "Pupils look real good there," she said. "Ah-huh, real good, Michelle. You know you have to eat, young lady."

She reached around and felt the back of my head and I let out a yelp.

This third grader with a blood-speckled cotton ball shoved up his nose stood in the doorway and ogled me. His curious blink overly animated behind his dense dorkville glasses.

"Joshua." Nurse Ample turned to the boy. "Come on, now." And she took his hand and hurried him off.

"How did you know I was here?" I asked Uncle Jack.

"They still had me down as your emergency contact."

"Sorry you had to leave school."

"It's all right. You're saving an entire period of seventh graders from dissection day." Uncle Jack grinned. "You skipped some meals, didn't you?" He pulled out a bag of protein treats from his briefcase. "How are things going over there?"

"How do you think? Super-great. Terrific," I said, looking away. "How could you tell him to stay?"

"I didn't. Here. Mickey, eat." Uncle Jack handed me a peanut butter cracker.

I propped myself up on my elbows and ate the cracker.

"He said he thought it would be best," said Uncle Jack.

"But you agreed. You know how he is. He's like a firecracker."

"Only if someone lights the fuse. Keep eating," he said, handing me another cracker. "And I didn't agree. I didn't disagree."

Uncle Jack passed me a Dixie cup with frolicking whitetailed bunnies on the outside.

"Don't you even wonder where he's been?" I asked, dribbling water onto my shirt. "Guess not, huh? Since you already knew where he was."

He lowered his head, taking the cup back.

"Eat this," he said.

I refused the cracker with my eyes staring at my sneakers.

"I've only known on and off. Your father thought it was best that if and when Danny wanted to contact you, Danny should be the one doing it."

"Dad knew? Is there anyone who *didn't* know besides me? Six years and as far as I was concerned he was dead and you said nothing. Not that I really care about him anyway, but I never thought you'd lie to me."

"It wasn't my place. It was Danny's. He's your brother—"

"Stop saying that. It's like it gives him some special pass at screw up. Anything else you wanna tell me? If the law's after him, maybe? I mean, something ain't right about him. I think it's the law."

"Why don't you ask him?"

" 'Cause I shouldn't have to. Besides, he's running. I can feel it all over him. He's hiding something. Something in Wisconsin."

"I don't know a lot about your brother. But you know what I always say, people deserve second chances. From the looks of Danny, he's due."

"So what? I'm stuck with him. You won't let me move back in?" I fell back onto the pillow. "This sucks."

I ran my hand over the bumps bubbling out of the white wall.

"Can't you give him a few days?" said Uncle Jack. "Maybe a week? It's nearly summer, Mickey."

Uncle Jack handed me another cracker, and I waved it away.

"Listen, you want to be angry with me, that's fair. I wish I had done different, but I couldn't. But you have to eat. Now sit up."

I raised up on my elbows again and took the cracker.

"I'm only a phone call away," he reassured me. "But I think you need to do this or you'll regret it later."

"Right . . ."

"Hey, there's already enough stuff that happens in life that you'll get down on yourself about that usually won't have anything to do with you, darlin'. This thing with Danny actually might."

I finished off the crackers and silky ice-cold water just about the time the bell over the door of the nurse's office clang-slammed, resonating a dull buzz. Christina shot in like a hysterical mother.

"I ditched PE as soon as I could. You okay?"

"You ditched PE 'cause I wasn't there to keep them distracted while you read—"

"Forget that. *Adio mio*, are you okay?" Her clammy hand clenched mine. "I totally lit three candles in my mind on the way here. What did they say?"

"I'm fine," I said. "It's not like they've given me three months to live. I just should've eaten."

Her worry flared to anger in a flash.

"*Adio mio*. Are you kidding me?" She slapped me on my shoulder. "You mean this is from you not eating? What did I tell you, Gringa? What?"

Uncle Jack cupped his hand over his mouth, hiding a smirk.

"I said, 'You eat, Gringa, or you'll get the shakes and pass out.' What are you trying to do? Leave me to sit outside the school dance next weekend with no one to talk to?"

"I thought we weren't going this year."

"It doesn't matter. Don't argue with me. I could've changed my mind. And there I'd be with no one to make fun of the anorexic cheerleaders arm-charming for the jock squad."

The doorbell ding-clanged again.

"I'm sorry, I'm sorry," I said.

"You better be, and don't go being all selfish again."

"Can't believe you walked all the way here," I said.

"Are you loco, Gringa? How hard you hit your head?" She reached for my head, and I flinched. "I hitched a ride."

I tipped my head around her and saw Ricky sitting in a chair right outside the room. He smiled at me, and I blushed from cheek to cheek.

"Oh my god, are you nuts?" I asked.

Uncle Jack tipped his head to see Ricky, who waved.

"Relax. He was gonna ditch anyway. Besides, I think he really likes you."

"Christina . . ."

"What? Like you couldn't tell in the car this morning—"

"Car?" interrupted Uncle Jack.

"Nothing," I finished.

"Hey, Mr. Johnson," Christina said as if just realizing Uncle Jack was sitting there. "Isn't this dissection day?"

"That's some memory of yours, Christina."

"No, I just have a niece in your class and she was ramming her finger down her throat all night so she could get out of it today." She turned her attention back to me. "So listen—"

"I have an idea," Uncle Jack said, standing up. "Christina, how about you head on back up to the high school? And take your accomplice with you. I'll call Sharon in the office and see if she'll excuse you."

"But—" she pleaded.

"Go," I said. "Last thing you need is to get grounded."

She leaned in and hugged me. "Don't do that again," she said. "I have to pray extra then. I'm trying to cut back you know."

"Go . . ."

Ricky held up his hand in an uncommitted wave as Uncle Jack nudged the two of them out. I fell back on the pillow, wincing on impact before tilting my head comfortably away from the bump toward that boy running with the dog. Nothing's that easy. They shouldn't set you up that way, to think it ever would be. I was thinking about ripping the poster off the wall when—

"You ready?" asked Uncle Jack.

"For what?" I said.

"To go home."

Danny had the truck hood open when Uncle Jack pulled up to the house. He poked his head out to see who it was, then jerked out of view. We sat in the car for a moment.

"Remember," said Uncle Jack. "Just tell him what you need, Mickey."

What I needed? I needed to get my clothes and books and drive off with Uncle Jack. That's what I needed.

"Come on," Uncle Jack said.

I walked a little light-legged from my spell earlier but got sturdier when we came up on Danny. We stood there a good five seconds as he tinkered with the radiator.

"This thing's a mess," he complained. "Just when one thing works another stops." He chucked the socket wrench in the toolbox. "Some kind of trouble?" he said, looking at Uncle Jack.

"She fainted."

Danny straightened out, wiping his oily hands on an old dishrag hanging from his jeans.

"You okay?" he asked, reaching to touch me.

I stepped back.

"She can't miss meals. You should know that," said Uncle Jack. "Hypoglycemia. Started a few years ago."

Danny looked at me hard like I'd set him up for that lecture.

"Well, I'm not gonna follow her around with a plate of food," he said. "Figure she's old enough to know what to do."

Uncle Jack was stumped for a moment. Danny picked through the toolbox.

"So you've settled on staying?" asked Uncle Jack.

"That still all right by you?" Danny said.

"Fine by me. Just realize that she may seem all grown up but she needs some looking after," said Uncle Jack. "That is why you're here."

Danny nodded and went back to the truck.

"Well, I better get on back up to the junior high." Uncle Jack hugged me real tight. "You call me if you need anything."

He waited for some kind of response from Danny, then made for his car.

"Jack?" Danny stepped out from under the hood. "Just kinda curious. Where's Sara? Things not work out between the two of you?"

A part of me thought Danny knew exactly where she was and that he brought it up to be hurtful. But who would've told him? I hadn't said a word about it.

Uncle Jack's shoulders sank more forward than usual. It was like watching something relaxed wad up. He cleared his throat as if trying to reach somewhere deep to put the words together. "Few years back, she was in an accident outside of Austin."

The repeating of any detail about how Aunt Sara died always took the life right out of him. It had been a little over two years, but he still talked about her like she was out doing errands or staying after school to grade papers. She wasn't dead. She was . . . preoccupied.

Danny bit on his lower lip and with the casualness of asking for a stick of gum said, "That's hard." And tucked himself back under the hood.

Hard? Was he serious? It was like he didn't know how to be respectful or caring or even human. There wasn't a person in town didn't drop at least one tear when they heard about Uncle Jack losing Aunt Sara the way he did. They'd been childhood sweethearts. Both of them teaching science at the junior high. Not to mention, she made a pie for Danny every birthday after Mom split. Big fluffy meringue with pastel sprinkles and crackling candles. On Parents' Night senior year, it was Aunt Sara and Uncle Jack who walked on the field with Danny 'cause of Dad being so—so—it didn't matter. What mattered was that Danny was straight up in the wrong, being that way with Uncle Jack. He had to have known it, and I couldn't figure why he still did it. Maybe he really was like people said after the stadium went, maybe he was crazy.

Uncle Jack smiled at me as he backed away toward his car. As I watched him, my stomach rolled into ten tight knots. He waited a moment before starting the ignition. Almost as if he forgot what came next before he finally pulled away.

I glared, and I mean glared, at Danny. It was one thing to be all cold about Dad. That was a given I guess, but to Uncle Jack? What was his damn dysfunction? He was like something that got picked up and dropped from a funnel cloud, shattered and scattered all over the place. Just looking at him made me want to come unglued.

He tucked his hair behind his ear. "What?"

I nodded my head and headed for the house.

"She died, Danny. Don't you have any kind of feeling about that?"

"What did you want me to say, Mickey?"

"Stop calling me that!" I said, slamming the screen door behind me.

I charged into my bedroom and sailed onto my bed. Of all the stupid luck to get stuck with Danny. Stuck with the biggest loser older brother in the history of big brothers, even counting Christina's, and they really sucked except for Hector.

I rolled over, facing the window. The curtains wafted and curved wide enough from a vagabond breeze to see Danny working on that old truck, tapping and tightening. Over and over, making a piercing racket. His greasy arms buried inside Dad's truck. Tapping and tapping . . . lulling me to sleep.

Danny shook me hard, waking me up in a damp puddle of drool that had soaked my pillowcase.

"You gonna sleep all afternoon?" he asked.

It was a little after five. Where did the last four hours go? I rolled over on my back as he stood at my bedside covered in grime. He reeked of gasoline and oil.

"Get out," I said, trying to orient myself.

"I knocked." He sat on the edge of my bed. "So . . ."

"What?"

"I figure if you're hyperglycemic—"

"Hypo," I corrected. "Hypoglycemic."

"Yeah, well, shouldn't you eat something? Around now?" he asked.

His eyes fell to the stack of books in the hollow of my nightstand.

"What are you looking at?" I scooted up against the headboard.

"The book," he said, nodding toward the stack. "Do you remember it?"

"Sitting there, isn't it?"

Danny slid *The Outsiders* from beneath the stack while I rubbed sleep from my eyes. He opened it, and it let out this real quiet crack. His hands glided along the pages and his eyes, those dark eyes, shifted in a magical movement. He drank in the words like it was the first water he'd run across in years. Danny's brow furrowed but his mouth made this way to smiling that, well, reminded me of that joke he made on The Stick. Only this time the smile didn't fade. It took and stuck and he really was in there.

He flipped to the back and saw the public library signature card. Written in cursive like the autograph of someone famous was *Danny Owens,* and tons of dates. Some of them spanning years.

"I stole it," I said.

Danny looked at me dumbfounded.

"Well, there was this boy freshman year who kept checking it out. So when it came back in, I took it. The library bought another one."

Danny nodded.

"You can borrow it. I mean, if you want," I said. "I don't really read it."

He smoothly ran his filthy hand along the cover. "So about this eating. Figure we could go get something after I shower. I mean, if you want."

"I don't have any money."

He shook his head. "I'm buying."

"Yeah, okay," I said.

And just like that, a boyish handsome smile cut the corners of his face. You would've thought the whole room lit up in just that second . . . like gold.

8

The bell over the Pizza Hut door dinged off-key as Danny and I walked in. A cluster of mostly teenage girls behind the register took to looking him over top to bottom to top real quick. Danny walked past the PLEASE WAIT TO BE SEATED sign and dived into a nonsmoking booth. He slid deep into the far corner with me awkwardly across from him. I glanced over my shoulder and saw the girls yank the menus back and forth, playfully squabbling over who'd get to serve us.

Had it been a Friday night during football season, there would barely have been standing room. The Pizza Hut was one of the few places where any kind of kid could hang out and for the most part fit in. Everyone was united in the excitement of the game. The talk of who was going out with who or who would hook up by the time they drove home. It was a tailgate party where the police turned a blind eye to a beer or two in the parking lot. Where the adults let things slide, especially in a good season, provided everyone showed up to Sunday church. Thankfully, that Friday wasn't football season and there were only a couple of overweight women falling out of their stretch pants huddled in a back booth. And a handful of kids playing video games behind us.

The waitress dropped the menus in front of us. A crooked glittery gold star pasted onto her name tag—Margarite—meant she was employee of the month.

"Something to drink?" Margarite asked.

You would've thought my brother was the missing Beatle the way she glowed at him. The one who sat at the back of the tour bus writing all the lyrics and letting John Lennon or Paul McCartney sign their names to them. You'd have thought Danny had been on the last cover of *GQ* or *Sports Illustrated* with a water-soaked ripped white T-shirt and a headline that sprayed across the page like MYSTERIOUS AND COOL. DANNY OWENS IS FAMOUS ON HIS OWN TURF with the Pirates' football stadium burnt to a crisp in the background and the state football trophy at his side. Only he wasn't famous. He was infamous.

"Beer," he said without a second thought.

Her eyes shifted to me to cue him, so she didn't have to say no.

"It's a dry county, remember?" I said. "They don't serve beer in the restaurants."

He squinted at the soda dispenser instead of reading the menu. "Coke. With lime—no, lemon. Yeah, that's fine."

"Sweet tea, lots of ice," I said as she hip-popped off.

Danny pulled out his cigarettes, pounding the pack on his callused palm. He dug into his jeans and slipped out Mr. Weldon's Zippo lighter. I felt the wind knock right out of me just looking at it but couldn't tell you why. I mean—he got it New Year's Eve 1998 when we were out in back of the hardware store picking up wood scraps for the bonfire that night. Mr. Weldon dipped out the side door and said he'd heard what the seven varsity seniors would be doing at the stadium after Roland's party.

"When you light up that ninety-eight tonight in the middle of the field," said Mr. Weldon, "the whole town will be behind you. Even if they call it hell-raising, you remember there ain't a man in this town that ain't proud of you boys. You done us all good. Especially you, Danny. We know you kept him grounded."

Mr. Weldon pressed the Zippo into Danny's strong hands. He told us how it had been custom-made for him when he went off to Vietnam. Its wide metal body was a silver mirror with a fourteen-karat-gold-rope trim cut in the markings of a rattlesnake. On one side, a raised impression of the Three Rivers Pirate, and the state of Texas on the other. It was some deal to give that to a boy who wasn't your own. Some kind of big deal, and Danny grinned ear to ear. He'd make them all proud.

Six years later the Zippo was tarnished and nicked. Part of the gold along the cap smashed into the silver. Danny popped the top, tipping his head and leaning in while in one movement he rolled his thumb on the wheel. Fire!

The orange-yellow glow sparked up the Marlboro and

added a wilder, angrier color to his face. He puff-puffed and the smoke trailed like a lazy day out from between his chapped lips. He looked at the flame for just a moment too long. Its flickering wave danced in his dark hollow eyes. The only evidence of warmth in them. He caught me staring, and I dropped my eyes to the menu real quick. I heard the snap-click of the lighter top striking shut, and he slipped it back in his pocket like neither one of us had seen nothing. Nothing at all but a guy lighting a cigarette. In the nonsmoking section.

He flipped the sugar packets out of the holder and made an ashtray. He tapped the ash off, pressing himself firm against the redbrick wall. His boots hanging over the edge of the booth. Smoke untangled from his lips in thick dense waves, breaking apart and scrambling at the light hanging over the table. He rolled the end of the cigarette against the sugar tray, watching these three kids behind us pound the heck out of a video game they didn't seem to have sunk a quarter into. One of those women in the back shouted in fast Spanish at the kids, and they peeled off, running toward her. One of them, a boy maybe seven, eight at the most, stopped right at the end of Danny's boots.

The boy giggled and said, "You got big shoes."

The woman spoke again and the boy shot off. Danny rolled around, sliding his feet under the table. He bit his lower lip, looking out the window, sucking in hard on that cigarette.

"What if Ponyboy grew up in *The Outsiders*?" he said, brushing his damp clean hair from his eyes.

"Can't happen," I told him.

"Why not? Everybody's gotta sometime," said Danny.

"That's why *The Outsiders* is so good. Kind of like *Peter Pan*. I mean, so Pony what, becomes the next John Grisham or worse, some lawyer type in a suit? No, Pony stays gold 'cause he's fourteen and he goes through hell and back but in the end, he's got his brothers and the gang. It's the best kind of dream."

"You wish you were Pony?" he said.

"It's a book. It isn't real."

The cherry started to bust off his cigarette, and he shoved it back on. "You were Pony."

"Not me," I said, fidgeting in my seat.

"What do you mean? You were Pony."

"I wanna grow up," I said.

He let out this breath that was a half laugh. "Yeah, seems you do."

"You know, you're not supposed to smoke here," I said.

Danny took a deep drag, his eyes holding steady on me. He smothered the cigarette in the sugar holder and slid it under the table.

We didn't really talk about much over dinner. He mentioned doing some dumb job out in Los Angeles and meeting a famous movie star that I hadn't heard of, but he said we'd watched all her movies growing up. I told him about the honors program and getting to leave school early at the end of May if things went right. It was an awkward kind of catch-up between garlic-cheese bread, Coke and sweet tea, and eventually pan pizza. For the most part, aside from the sometimes nervous crack of his neck or foot shaking under the table, there were glimpses of the old Danny before the fire. Before all the smoke.

When we got down to the last slice of pepperoni with extra cheese, he offered it up in a silly playful ceremony.

"In honor of Michelle being so big-brained and in spite of her poor choice in jeans."

"Shut up," I said.

"We bestow this final slice of pizza, straight from the ovens of small-town nowhere Texas to Ms. Michelle Owens. The smartest girl in three counties and maybe four."

I shoved it back at him. "You're so weird."

"Maybe," he said, sucking the red plastic Coke cup empty. "But I got you to laugh."

I swallowed the smile.

"Whaddya say I try to get you one of them stuffed animals out of that machine over there?" he said. "Come on, I'll pay and get you one. What?"

"Danny, I'm seventeen. . . ."

"So? The stuffed animal police is gonna bust you for being too old? You always liked those things."

Before I went any further, the doorbell dinged and Chuck Nelson and his trio of Letterman Lizards rolled in. They were the worst kind of guys to run into at the Pizza Hut. Their hearts were lined with blue ribbons, all-star medals, Abercrombie & Fitch, and the girls they'd slept with or said they had. They were worse than the meth dealers or the small-time gangster wannabes. Guys like Chuck and his friends were white wealthy rednecks who liked to raise hell twice on Sunday and made sure you never forgot your place on or off the field. Not to mention Chuck hated me . . . to the nth degree.

"I just wanna go," I said.

"Oh come on," said Danny, leaving the tip. "I'll pay and getcha one fast."

Chuck's eyes hung on us as one of the waitresses took them to a booth.

"Something wrong?" Danny asked, noticing me looking at Chuck.

"No."

When we got up to the counter, Danny seemed cheerful. Even grinned in my direction. Then it happened. As quick as a needle gets lost in the carpet, his expression shifted. The color drained right from his face when he saw a bunch of framed newspaper clippings on the wall beside the register. His eyes held firm on the team photo with the headline: PIRATES STATE ALL STARS SEASON '98. There wasn't a place in town that didn't have some kind of shrine to that magical year, in spite of what followed. And there on the wall of the Pizza Hut was one clipping after another, as if they'd suddenly manifested for him to look at.

Margarite held out his change. "Sir?"

"Danny?" I said.

He shook his head and steeled his eyes. Cracked his neck and took the money from her. As he stuffed it back in his wallet, I saw a picture of a woman. Christina would've said she looked famous too.

"Who's that?" I asked.

"Come on," he said, with his eyes still on the wall.

We'd nearly made it to the door when that stupid claw

machine made an astro-noise, yanking him back. I sighed, looking over at Chuck and the Lizards ordering.

"It's really not that big of a deal, Danny."

He sank in a dollar and the carnival music revved up.

"I said I'd get you something."

His eyes squinted like he was looking down the sights of a shotgun. His hand popped the lever in quick precise movements. Chuck peered around the booth. The machine claw dropped. It fastened onto a brown plush teddy bear. The bear sailed along, then slipped off just before the release hatch.

"Dammit," Danny said.

He was pissed. A weird kind of pissed about something bigger than the fifty-cent toy he was after. He shoved another dollar bill in the machine.

The Lizards cackled. Chuck smirked.

"Forget it. Let's just go," I said.

"I can get it," he said with his eyes narrowing again.

His face burned. His hand, more tense, squeezed the lever, causing the claw to jerk and bobble. He went for the same stuffed animal. This time the claw missed altogether.

"Shit," he said, smacking the Plexiglas wall of the machine.

The whole game shook, and I stepped back a little bit. Danny stared at that bear and dug deep into his pocket and unwadded another dollar bill. He shoved it in, and the slot spit it out.

"Let's just go," I pleaded.

"I can get it."

He ran the dollar over the edge of the game, smoothing

out the creases. The girls behind the register stared. The group of dumb jocks with their cocky smirks stared. Even the stupid framed newspaper clippings were watching us. Not again. No way was I going through it all again. The whispers, the stares, all the questions about Danny and if I was in some way gonna be as crazy as him 'cause I'd seen it too. I'd seen what happened even if—if . . .

No damn way was I doing it all again, so I took off out the door, dinging that stupid bell hard. I climbed in the truck and snapped the lap belt on tight.

After about ten years, Danny came out of the Pizza Hut and got in the truck empty-handed. "I just wanted to give you something," he said.

I shook my head. "Just go."

"What's wrong with you?"

"I'll tell you what's wrong with me. You seen those guys that came in? Monday at school, I gotta hear about my brother flippin' out over some stupid teddy bear."

"I'm sure it's not a big deal," he said.

"Nothing is to you. You come. You go. There's no consequence."

"You want me to go talk to 'em," he said with his foot halfway out the truck, "I will."

"No. Dontcha get it? I don't want you to talk to anyone. Okay? Just leave it be."

He eased back into the truck, quietly shutting the door behind him.

"I thought we were doing okay," he said.

"Just take me home."

9

The howl of the six-thirty train whistle woke me up the next morning. I laid there for a moment watching the wheat-colored sun smile through the bottom of the curtain, illuminating the dancing specks of dust quickly vanishing in the darkness of the rest of the room. I was tired after a night of bad dreams, and the thought of getting up and sitting in class at the community college some sixty miles away sank me a little deeper into the soft mattress. I had dozed back off only for a couple minutes when the smells of buttermilk pancakes and fried ham steaks swam over me. I stretched out as far as I could and wondered why the heck my brother was up so early on a Saturday. Half hoping this was his attempt at a farewell breakfast.

I stepped into a faded pair of Lees and punched my tired arms into a boyish button-down. My stomach growled, believing the smell was some indication of a digestible meal.

In the kitchen, Danny half danced while flipping pancakes in the skillet. I tossed my books on the kitchen table and poured a glass of OJ.

"Thought you might want some breakfast," he said. "Wouldn't be cool to have you passing out in front of college kids."

"Right . . . ," I said.

He lifted the lid off the frying pan and a burst of steam spit up. The potatoes crackled as he shuffled them with the spatula. My mouth salivated at the smell of fried onions and home fries.

"Since when can you cook?" I asked.

"Um, since I was in Arizona a couple of years ago with three dollars in quarters in my pocket and a hangover from hell. I was either gonna steal my next meal or take a job at the restaurant I was eating at as a dishwasher. You didn't think I screwed up every meal, did ya?"

He flipped a pancake in the air and caught it in the pan. "The cook, Harvey, he'd been in that grease dump for fourteen years, and man, did he look it. Funny fella with a real high-pitched voice and a big old flabby body, and he smelled like sour milk and chili. He was getting so fat he couldn't stand for too long. So he started teaching me how to cook."

He slid the pancake out of the skillet and into a stack in the oven.

"The restaurant was right off the interstate in the middle of nothing, so there was always some pack of truckers at the counter telling their tall tales about a sixteen-hour shift. A bunch of kids on their way to the Grand Canyon taking pictures of every rock they saw. Little old ladies played cards in the back for hours and hours, sipping sweet lemonade or decaf. One thing about that dump, you were never alone."

"You like it? Arizona?" I asked.

"As much as anywhere, I guess," he said.

"Why didn't you stick?"

"Look at this." He scooped a fluffy cheese omelet onto a plate. "Nice, huh?"

He shoveled on a side of home fries and a golden brown short stack. It was right out of a Denny's commercial. He placed it all in front of me and my whimpering stomach.

"I can't eat all this," I said.

"Good." He scooted a chair up next to me. "I was planning on splitting it with you."

He sliced the omelet in half and gooey cheese oozed onto the scuffed-up white plate.

"What do you think?" he asked.

"Not bad," I said, with a mouthful of omelet. "It's actually kind of okay."

His face relaxed a little. As if my approval was of some kind of importance. Truth was, it was all damn good.

"Listen. I'm real sorry about last night," Danny said. "I—didn't mean to . . . I didn't mean to scare you or embarrass you or . . . you know?"

I kept my head down splitting off a bite of pancakes with my fork.

"Forget it," I said.

I sure wanted to, but knowing Chuck and his posse, that wasn't going to be easy.

"Listen," Danny said. "I spoke with Jack last night when we first came home. And I'm gonna run you over to college today."

"No way. No," I said, dropping my fork.

"Why not? Hell, I drove you all over this state one time or another."

"This is important to me, Danny. I have to be on time and someone has to pick me up."

"I'm sure it ain't brain surgery," he said.

"No, it's harder. You have to be there."

I cut him to the quick and didn't much care. I had worked hard all these years in school while he was out dishwashing or hell-raising. Now he wanted to step in and be big brother, a job as far as I was concerned he wasn't qualified for.

"Michelle, why you gotta make everything so hard? I mean, here I am offering."

"Give me the keys, then," I said. "I got a license—"

"I can do this. I can be here—there."

Danny saying he'd be there was like the president saying "Read my lips. No new taxes," when you damn well knew that there would be more taxes. With Danny, there would be more everything, like lying, like not saying anything at all. There I'd be, standing in the college parking lot almost sixty miles away from home wondering how I could've let him talk me into it.

"All right." He set the keys on the table. "You know, you're grown enough. Do what you think's best."

All I had to do was pick up those keys. After my classes, I could go anywhere. I could get as far, or at least seventy-miles-an-hour as fast, from Danny—from Three Rivers, from the smell of smoke. The smoke that I could never wash off my skin—my clothes—all I had to do was pick up those keys. Pick up those keys and vanish. The thought suddenly sent a brick of fear right into my gut.

What was I thinking? Disappear?

"You better be there," I said.

I picked up my fork and kept eating.

Community college was nothing like Three Rivers High. There weren't any bells herding the students into class like mindless sheep. No shaming looks if you didn't write down what the teacher had to say. College was great because you were almost invisible, and it was all on you to show up with your homework done, ask the right questions and, if at all possible, be awake.

The college kids who sat with sixty-four-ounce Mountain Dews in my eight o'clock math class were too tired or too hung over to really care that I was a seventeen-year-old high school junior. They didn't care that my dad used to be a drunk and my mom ran off partly out of boredom and partly because of manic depression. They didn't care about Danny, or Roland dying, or the state football trophy. All they wanted, most of them, was to stay awake and earn their three credits. And I got to be just another body filling a plastic-backed seat next to them.

It was the best place I had been to in the last six years.

After classes, I sat in a stall in the women's restroom for a little over twenty minutes. I worked out all the scenarios of how Danny wouldn't be there when I first got out so why rush? How it just made it easier to psych myself up for the disappointment, for the reality of Danny. A couple of girls floated in, touching up their makeup, chitchatting about going to a party later. I watched their shapely bodies in tight jeans and fitted short-sleeve shirts through the space along the stall door. They were maybe a year or two older than me, but they were women. Everything about them was feminine and experienced and beautiful. I looked down at my lousy ensemble and pulled my feet a little tighter under me on the toilet seat.

Once the girls were gone, I stepped out of the stall. I splashed water on my face before realizing there weren't any paper towels, so I used my shirttails. What was meant to be a quick look in the mirror became something I couldn't ever remember doing before. I stared at the deep brown-blackness of my eyes. How they cut in sharp at the edges. The lashes were all long and girly, and there I was thinking that couldn't be me. I'm not girly. I'm not feminine. My jaw was soft, so I clenched my teeth. There I was.

That was me.

I made my way down the corridor toward the doors leading to the parking lot. It was quiet aside from passing the occasional lecture in one of the classrooms. No hallway lockers. Just doors. Doors and big glass windows.

At the end of the hall, I shoved the metal door bar and didn't raise my head until I got to the bottom of the concrete steps. There he was, sitting on the toolbox of the truck, reading *The Outsiders*. A part of me wanted to run right back inside, call Uncle Jack and beg him to come get me 'cause it half scared me, Danny being there waiting for me.

He folded the book closed and slipped it into his back pocket.

"Sorry I'm late," I said.

"It's cool. Nice day to take in the sun anyhow." He hopped over the tailgate. "You learn anything you didn't already know?"

"Yeah," I said.

"Maybe you could tell me about it later," he said, opening the driver's door.

I got in the truck and put my books between us.

He turned over the ignition and the big ol' engine sounded cherry mint as he revved it. Then he let it settle.

"You really didn't think I'd show, did ya?"

I dropped my eyes to the rolled-down window.

"There's a DQ round the corner," I said.

"Yeah, I seen it when I was waiting."

We both sat there waiting for the other one to state the obvious. He wasn't gonna bend, and I was starving.

"Maybe we could pick up something before we headed home," I said. "If you want."

"Sure." He nodded and dropped the gear into drive.

We drove over the black rubber tube at the Dairy Queen drive-thru and stopped just shy of the speaker box. He dug into his haggard Levi's and came out with that lighter. He dipped the filter of a Marlboro Red between his lips.

"What do you want—"

"Welcome to Dairy Queen home of the Beltbuster," the intercom voice said. "Would you like to try one of our delicious Combo Meals today?"

"Yeah, um . . . one cheeseburger, everything on it. A large chili fry and a extra large strawberry shake." He dropped his head over to me. "What do you think?"

"Will that be all, sir?" the voice said.

"A cheeseburger—" I said.

"Yeah, another cheeseburger," he repeated, and before I could finish, "with mayo and extra mustard and no onions. And a large Coke. Vanilla Coke."

He looked back at me for confirmation. His eyes were a softer brown than before.

"You like Vanilla Coke still, dontcha?" he asked.

"Yeah, I still like it."

"Is that all, sir?" the voice asked.

"Yeah," he said to the intercom.

He exhaled a smooth line of smoke, seeming very proud of himself.

"Hey, I got something right, huh?"

He had.

10

Christina flung a plastic bag full of Styrofoam containers though my bedroom window around five that evening.

"Pull me in," she said, struggling to lift herself inside.

I grabbed ahold of her arms and pulled. I slipped forward and she fell back onto the grass.

"Real funny, Gringa."

"You could've come in the front door," I said as she made her way back up to the windowsill.

"Watch the Coke," she said. "Besides, I didn't know what kind of mood your brother would be in. Pull."

Christina's diet of enchiladas, rice, and beans had managed to weigh her down over the last year. Not that she was ever really skinny. I grunted and heaved her in as she flopped to the floor.

"What kind of mood is he in?" she asked.

"Relax, he's asleep. Does your mom know you're here?"

"Nope. She got one of her headaches and went to that witch doctor woman on the other side of the river. I swear that woman creeps me out."

"Your mom or the witch?"

"Both I guess," she said, untying the bag. "So, did he beat up any inanimate objects today?"

"Ha, ha. Who told you?"

"You're kidding, right? You know how gossip spreads around here. I probably knew about it before you almost broke the Pizza Hut door storming out."

"It wasn't like that," I said.

Even though it kind of was and the distorted version of what happened would be all over school Monday morning. Yet one more thing for Chuck Nelson and the Letterman Lizards to hassle me about. Like it wasn't enough to just outright be mean 'cause Chuck and me actually had a history, sort of.

"Can we talk about something else?" I asked.

"Okay, how was college?"

"Okay. Danny drove me and managed to actually pick me up on time."

"Oh yeah . . . so maybe he's not so bad," she said.

Whatever. It would take a lot more than a ride to make my brother anywhere close to not so bad.

"Damn, Gringa. I don't want to bring you down, but you look like crap."

"Yeah, still not really sleeping."

"What did I tell you? Crack an egg and put it in vinegar under your bed. Or is it don't crack it? Let me ask my cousin again. She always has that sleeping problem after she gets dumped." She opened a lid dripping with water beads. "Want some?"

I stared at the heaping mountain of nachos covered in greasy meat, beans, white cheese, guacamole and jalapeños.

"I'm not hungry."

She slugged me in the arm. "Get hungry. You're not pulling that fainting thing on me again."

I dug a nacho out as she unwrapped a tinfoil roll of tortillas for a container full of chicken and beef fajitas.

"So, I had that house dream again last night."

She loaded up a tortilla with guacamole and sour cream. "Go ahead."

"The floors were polished redwood this time. The kitchen was maybe three times as big as this room."

"That's big," she said, layering the fajita meat.

"The pots and pans were shiny clean and everything was where it oughta be. There was a dog out back—"

"What kind?" she asked.

"A gold Lab; and a mom and a dad."

"Your mom?"

"No, just some mom, but she was mine in the dream. She had on this soft yellow sundress and her smile . . . it made me feel real easy inside. We ate at the dinner table and we talked about things that were on our minds. Ate good food. Pot roast, I think. And green bean casserole, honey-dipped biscuits and fresh fruit salad. There was just this feeling that no one went away for longer than a trip to the store or work or school. There was this feeling . . ." I struggled to find the words.

"What?" Christina asked.

"Like home. For the first time, the dream felt like home."

She wiped her mouth on a napkin. "Look, I know you don't believe me, but that whole eating at the table isn't as romantically *Brady Bunch* as you think, Gringa. In my house, it's a cross between a beauty shop gossip session and a public attack if you eat too much or too little. Trust me, be glad you haven't been tormented every day of your life." She bit into her fajita taco. "So, how did it end? Did you marry Johnny Depp again? Damn, he's hot. Even if he's part *gringo*."

"No, um . . . There were these fireworks that I could see outside my bedroom window. Shimmering blues and reds, silvers and golds, piercing the black sky. Then it's on fire."

"The sky?" she asked.

"No, the house."

I paused as the hair on my arms stood straight up. A dense rush of adrenaline reminded me how hot I had felt in the dream.

"The paint peeled off the walls of my bedroom. There were these swells of orange-yellow swimming across the ceiling. I couldn't say anything—I couldn't breathe. I wanted out. Out of the house. Out of my skin soaked in sweat and the heat that . . ." I drifted for a moment. "Everyone gets out. Even the dog. Everyone but me. And Danny's standing in the front yard, watching it burn. With his eyes all . . . I don't know. Empty."

"Damn, Gringa," she said, biting into a nacho. "I know

93

you don't trust him, but to think he'd set you on fire. I mean, come on. Be pissed at him for ditching you, but that stadium thing wasn't his fault. If it were, he'd be doing time. Right?"

I shrugged.

"I mean, I know you don't like to talk about it—"

"I don't. Wanna talk about it."

Christina pursed her lips and sucked on her straw.

"It's just a stupid dream," I said.

"That's why you have it all the time, right? Not that the version with Johnny Depp isn't totally cool, I mean, but maybe you're remembering something. You said you don't really remember—"

"Christina, stop, okay? I don't need the headshrinker crap. What happened is over."

"Fine," she said, dropping it.

I had learned not to think about that night. It didn't change anything to think about it. It didn't—I don't know. It just made me feel a hole or a loneliness or a whole list of other crap that made my mind spin counterclockwise. I didn't like that feeling. I didn't like feeling. I couldn't tell her that though.

"But you know what?" I said.

Christina shook her head, chewing a nacho.

"Danny's hiding something. He got this letter from Wisconsin the day after he got here and acted all weird when he knew I saw it."

"Wisconsin? Wow, I thought you just saw it on the map one day," she said, catching me in a lie. "Anyways, did you ask him about it?"

I shrugged. "Not really."

"I'll tell you something, Gringa. I think he's innocent. All people are innocent until proven guilty. Even if they're *gringos*. Not that I'm racist."

"Sure," I said, fingering a nacho.

"Okay, enough *loco* dreams and suspicious brother talk. Ask me why I'm here. Come on." She bumped me with her shoulder. "You wanna ask me."

"Why are you here, Christina?"

"Okay, that was a totally weak effort *but* I'm going to tell you anyway. Ricky came in the restaurant asking about you."

She crunched into a nacho, plopping globs of guacamole along her knuckles.

"Whatever," I said, butterflies fluttering in my stomach.

"Gringa, I am so serious. So here's the scenario. Ricky comes in with Johnny Lee and sits in my section, right. Which totally pissed off Angie. Like I told you, she's got that crush on him, which, if you ask me, is totally gross 'cause she's nineteen and a half which is almost twenty and he's what, like barely eighteen 'cause of that whole flunkie thing."

"Get to the point," I said.

"Calm down. So he's in my section and he's like 'So, Christina, you think Mickey would go out with me?' "

"Shut up! No f-ing way."

"Oh my God and three saints did I just want to stick my tongue out at Angie." Christina stuck out her tongue, laughing. "She was all big-eyeing us from the register and you could smell her being pissed like one of them stray dogs that rolls around on a dead fish."

"And . . . ? What did you say?" I could barely sit still.

"Hold on. I'm starving." She swallowed a mouthful of

95

tortilla and fajitas. "Okay, anyway, I said, 'Like, I don't know, why don't you just ask her out?' And he said it was complicated and that he thought maybe you liked him but he wasn't sure." Christina slurped her Coke. "What's wrong?"

"Maybe it's all a prank. I mean, come on, Ricky Martinez and me? I mean, seriously," I said, crawling up on my bed.

"You see, you're doing that thing again. That thing where you start being negative." Christina pushed me over and lay beside me. "He's a nice guy. Not like most of the machismo baby-makers around here. And you haven't had a boyfriend in, let's see . . . *never!*"

"Shut up," I said, nudging her.

She nudged back and started a shoving war. "Gringa, don't make me push you off your own bed."

Just then I rammed right into her, and she pounded onto the floor. It was fun to laugh for a second. To just be a teenager and talk about boys and nothing too serious. Then I felt guilty, remembering Dad. Dad just being buried Wednesday and there it was Saturday and I hadn't even thought about going out to the cemetery once. I drew back my smile.

"Hey," she said.

"What?"

"You know, there's only so much bad that can happen to a person. Then it just has to average out."

I nodded.

"So maybe you don't want to and really shouldn't hook up with anyone right now. That doesn't mean you can't be a little high that Ricky 'The Ghost' Martinez likes you."

"Yeah, maybe."

I got up and sat in the windowsill. It was minutes from sunset and my favorite part of every day. The copper-orange tint lapped along the rooftops and revived the dead grass in the front yard into luscious patches of almond, sprinkled with lime spears. Dogs barked down the street and the neighbor's wind chimes' slender silver bodies tapped gently against each other. It was the kind of gold that Ponyboy talked about to Johnny in *The Outsiders*. The kind that filled you from the inside and made even the ugliest things seem brand-new. In that kind of sun, even the run-down houses on the corner somehow became restored. At that time of day, fathers didn't die and brothers didn't leave. Mothers were home and kids laughed at some silly sitcom on TV. Maybe it wasn't *The Outsiders'* sun exactly, but it sure made the whole block peaceful and lovely. Even if only for five or ten minutes out of a whole day.

Christina propped her elbows on the window ledge across from me. "Can you believe it, Gringa? How beautiful a town like this can look at this time of day. It's some kind of divine miracle, my mother would say."

She couldn't see my eyes watering up even though I knew I wouldn't cry. She couldn't feel what it was like to be so alone even with your best friend right beside you.

"I think your brother's innocent, Gringa, you know? And whatever you think he's not telling you, just ask him." She sucked her Coke dry. "Besides, doesn't he seem like he's gotta be famous for something somewhere?"

I sucked in a deep breath, as deep as it would go. "I don't know."

11

Danny pulled into the H-E-B parking lot so we could pick
up a pie to take over to Uncle Jack's. He'd called and invited
both of us over that morning for a Sunday barbecue. Before
we got out of the truck, Danny checked his wallet. He had
several hundred-dollar bills in there.

"Where'd you get all that?"

He slid it into his back pocket.

"Where everyone gets their money—"and he held a long
pause—"the ATM. Come on."

The doors squeaked as we hopped out.

"Gotta get some grease for the doors later. Don't let me
forget," he said.

Once inside, we walked past aisle after aisle of Sunday church traffic. Eyes shifted. I could feel them and even though he didn't say a word, I think he could too. Just by the way his shoulders stiffened and his eyes stayed forward.

"You think we should get ice cream?" he said, without looking at me trailing behind, wishing I were completely invisible.

"No, he'll have it."

We finally got to the bakery. He circled the table of pies.

"What do you think he'd wanna eat?" Danny said.

I crossed my arms over my stomach, trying not to notice the occasional stare or pointing—whispering. But it all felt so amplified.

"Mickey?" Danny said.

"I don't know. Apple, I guess."

"Apple, huh?" He raised his head and saw what I'd been seeing.

Danny huffed and bit on his lower lip. He picked up an apple pie, still perusing the coconut and pecan ones.

"People are staring—" I said.

"I *know*." And his tone sent a shiver up me. "I'm not gonna be chased outta here. Understand?"

I started looking anywhere but in his direction. Maybe people wouldn't even notice I was with him. That was nuts. Of course they would. They noticed everything in Three Rivers. My heart raced. My breath shortened. I wanted out of there. Then. Right then!

"Just get the damn pie, Danny. Okay?" I snapped.

He looked up at me and that darkness, it was there in his

eyes, all right. That black oil staring back at me made me think I'd combust on the spot.

"Fine," he said.

We got up to the register and the checkout lady, Mrs. Cortez, she recognized Danny right off. Of course she did. Not only did her son play football with him, but Danny might as well have been walking around with the word KILLER branded across his forehead. She swiped the bottom of the pie over the scanner.

"Four seventy-five," she said.

He handed her a hundred-dollar bill. She ran the counterfeit marker over it. When she tried to make change, she came up short. Dammit!

"I'll be back," she said.

She locked the register and went to the service counter.

"Couldn't you've given her a twenty?" I said.

"Could you give me a little less attitude?" he snapped.

"Whatever," I said under my breath.

That was when it happened.

"Danny Owens," a hefty voice said from behind me.

We both turned and saw Joe Sanchez. Big Junk-Head Joe, that's what they useta call him that year when the team went to state. Now he was just Fat Junk-Head Joe with three kids and a wife that hated him.

"Never thought I'd see you in Three Rivers again. People said you were dead."

"Yeah," Danny said, looking nervous. The kind of nervous he got before getting into a fight. "People say a lot of things, I guess. Keeps them busy."

"Yeah, somebody even said you tried to kill yourself." Fat

Junk-Head Joe kind of chuckled. "That you were in one of those loony bins up in Amarillo."

Danny didn't say anything. Just looked down at the bar-code scanner.

Mrs. Cortez stepped back behind the register and set up the drawer with her change. She counted it back out to Danny, whose hand was shaking something bad. I stepped around him and grabbed the plastic sack with the pie.

"So I guess you won't be here for very long," Fat Junk-Head Joe said to Danny.

"Oh yeah, why is that?" Danny challenged.

"Let's just go," I said to Danny.

"Well, you only killed your best friend—"

And before that meat-brain could get another word out, Danny ripped right for him. Slamming that slab of lard against the candy bars and bubble gum, then back into the tabloid magazines.

"Danny!" I shouted.

"You wanna make me run, Big Joe?" Danny said, squeezing his blubber neck. "You wanna?"

And Fat Junk-Head Joe just held his hands up. Something must've clicked in Danny's brain 'cause he real-ized that, like on TV, everyone had stopped moving. They were all watching him, waiting. Waiting to see it this time.

Danny shoved Fat Junk-Head Joe and backed away, never taking his eyes off him before leaving me there. Mrs. Cortez looked at me like, *you poor thing.* Dammit! I wanted to kill Danny.

I chased after him, heading for the truck.

"You couldn't let it slide. You never can just let things go."

He spun around, and I froze.

"You don't know what you're talking about, Michelle. You hear? You don't, so back off."

He dove into the truck and cranked up the engine. Lit a cigarette and pulled *The Outsiders* from the glove box. I stood there not knowing what to do. So I waited. And waited until he'd nearly smoked the cigarette to a butt. He flicked it out the window and threw the book back in the glove box, motioning me to get in.

Good thing we hadn't gotten ice cream.

Danny's knuckles lightly rapped on the whitewood screen door. I stood behind him with the store-bought apple pie in the plastic sack.

"Jack," Danny called through the door. He turned to me. "Do we just go in?" I stared at the porch floor.

"Michelle, I said I was sorry."

"Right . . ."

"Hey," said Uncle Jack from the kitchen, waving us in with a pair of tongs. "Come on in. Just gonna throw a plate of burgers and ribs on the grill."

The back door slapped behind Uncle Jack just as we came in the front. I walked across the hardwood living room floor onto the quarter-sized black-and-white tiled kitchen. He had a gigantic bowl of salad already in the making on the table. I fished out a cucumber dripping with red vinegar and slid the pie we had brought onto the countertop. Aside from a dishcloth here or there, Uncle Jack had kept the house exactly as it had been when Aunt Sara was living.

"You want something to drink?" I asked Danny.

I popped open a can of Pepsi from the fridge. When Danny didn't answer, I poked my head around the kitchen doorway and saw him looking at the mantel above the pretend fireplace. There were collages and multipicture frames with photos of Aunt Sara and Uncle Jack from all over the world. She loved to travel like nobody I'd ever met. Uncle Jack said she should've taught history, not science, so they could've written off their trips to the Aztec ruins or the gardens of Japan. And she was big on photos. Not like our parents. Up until I moved back in with Dad a little over a year ago, there had never been a picture of Danny or me—of any of us—up in our house. But in Aunt Sara's house, she celebrated the two of us like we were her own kids and always kept pictures of us up.

There was one with Danny holding me on his shoulders, me missing my two front teeth, Mom's feet in the background. Another of all of us, including Dad and Mom, at a barbecue at Uncle Jack's. Mom, with her eyes closed, swaying with a margarita in one hand and the other raised to the sky. Danny's football picture from senior year was next to that one. The medal he got for being all-state hung alongside it with the ribbons I won in band before I quit.

Danny reached for the framed clipping of Roland and him holding the state trophy. Both of them with the goofiest smiles, the headline read: FULL SCHOLARSHIP FOR GONZALEZ AND OWENS TO PLAY AT THE UNIVERSITY OF TEXAS.

"She never took any of it down," I said. "Not even when you were in juvie waiting for the trial and people would come around saying she should."

He stared at the picture frame. "Why would she keep all this?"

"You mean because of the way you treated her? How you stopped talking to her—acted like she didn't exist after all she'd done for you? Yeah, I don't know, Danny. I'm pretty stumped on that one."

"Things were confusing, Michelle."

"She never stopped believing in you, I guess."

He turned to me. "You?"

"I told her she should've taken them down."

"Huh." He looked around the room. "Everything's the same. Just the way I remember. The bowl on the coffee table full of those little slips of paper." He put the frame back on the mantel. "Remember she wrote them up and called them fortune cookie thoughts 'cause you always liked wise sayings."

He fished one out.

"What's it say?" I asked.

" 'You will be one of those people who goes places in life.' " He looked back at the mantel. "The places part isn't far off."

He folded the slip and shuffled it back in the bowl.

Uncle Jack came in the back door, eagerly snapping his tongs. "We got one heck of a meal cooking," he said.

I walked back into the kitchen.

"Hey, girl." And he gave me one of those famous Uncle Jack hugs that spilled goodness all over you. "Where's your brother?"

I motioned toward the living room just as the front screen door clicked shut.

"Something wrong?" he asked.

"I don't know. Seemed as fine as Danny ever is until he started looking at the pictures. And we had a little run-in at the grocery store, but it was no big deal."

"What kind of run-in? Mickey?"

"Just Fat Junk-Head Joe, who I'd say is pretty like-minded with me."

"Meaning?"

"Meaning you don't just come back to town after what Danny did."

"You can't give him a break, can you?"

I looked away.

"Hey." He lifted my chin, but I wouldn't look at him. "Okay." He let go and slid the tongs onto the counter. He heaved a heavy sigh. "I should've taken the pictures down, but I just couldn't."

"I know."

"Well, I guess I better talk to him."

Uncle Jack was midway across the living room when I said, "No. You got a lot of cooking to do. I'll go."

I was headed for the front door when he pulled me back. "Come here." He held me tight again. "You sure?"

"Yeah. He's my brother, right?"

"Go on," he said, making his way back into the kitchen. "Holler if you need me."

I threw a thumbs-up and stretched into a tight-lipped smile. Why wasn't I already hollering?

Danny was sitting on the front porch steps with a lit cigarette when I came out the screen door. He looked back, then away. "I'll be in in a minute," he said.

"Figured you might be planning your next disappearing act."

He shook his head. "I might stay just to spite you," he said. "Wouldn't that be something?"

"You okay?" I said.

"Yeah." His voice shook.

He drew a deep inhale on his cigarette, holding it in his lungs unusually long before letting it go.

"She was a good woman, huh?" he said.

"The best," I said. "She made pies for your birthday even after you left town. Guess just in case you ever decided to come back."

"Were you living here when she . . . when it happened?"

"No."

He flicked the ash off his cigarette and took another drag. I could hear the pop-crackle of the burning end even from where I was standing.

"It's complicated," he said, exhaling a V of smoke. "The last few years."

"I ain't asking."

"You ain't?" he said, turning to me.

I shook my head.

Danny rested his forehead in his palm. He took a drag, stamped the cigarette out on the underside of the porch step and dropped the butt in his Marlboro box. Standing up, he drew in a deep breath and shook himself off like a wet dog while he exhaled. His boot heels drummed on the gray-blue wooden porch as he walked past me. He stood there with the screen door open for a moment.

"You coming with?" he said.

The way he asked seemed like it mattered somehow. I turned and followed him inside.

Danny seemed more at ease that afternoon, helping Uncle Jack with the grill. The two of them sipped on bottles of ice-cold root beer, talking about something each of them had read in the newspaper. I didn't sit on the sidelines altogether, but it was better not to be smack in the middle of things for once.

When it came time to eat, we had one of those cheesy TV family afternoons.

We all sat around a picnic table with piles of mustard potato salad, roasted corn on the cob, sausage, burgers and fiesta salad covering our plates. Warm dinner rolls filled a big glass bowl lined with paper towels and each of us had a humongous glass of sweet sun tea. If somebody had driven by and seen us, I bet we would've looked like the family they always wanted. Almost.

On the way back to town from Uncle Jack's, the truck died on us. We lifted the hood and between the two of us agreed it was an easy fix, but Trevino's was closed. Danny was sure it wouldn't take over an hour once we got the part, so he pushed the truck to the side of the road while I steered. He grabbed his jean jacket from the cab and *The Outsiders* from the glove box. We stuck out our thumbs as we headed for town a few miles away.

He folded over the cover as we walked, reading to himself.

"What part are you at?" I asked.

"The part where Johnny wants to go back and turn himself in for killing the rich kid."

"Isn't that where you were yesterday?" I said. "I saw the place marking it, that's all."

"I don't like to read the end, so I skip around. Read the parts I like again."

"That's a weird way to read a book," I said.

"Really. How come?" he asked, closing it.

"Guess 'cause the story doesn't make as much sense broken into parts. I mean, you don't get why it's so important that Ponyboy is told to stay gold unless you read the part about them in Windrixville. You can't understand at the end why Pony's got to write the whole story if you don't know what it meant to lose so much to get to that point. I mean, how can you get the feeling of beginning again if you don't read the end?"

"Thought you didn't read it anymore," he said.

"I don't."

"Huh. How about we start it from the beginning sometime? You and me, like we used to."

I sat on my answer, not knowing how to make it hatch. Me and Danny sitting around as he read that book seemed about as crazy as everything about him now. His eyes fixed on me for a response.

"I don't know," I said.

"Okay. Guess you'll let me know if you change your mind."

I shrugged a maybe and he went back to reading.

The trouble started right from the moment we opened the door to Atkin's Autoparts. The last person you want to see always seems to be the first you run into, especially in a small town. Danny's luck had been running pretty smooth until that run-in with Fat Junk-Head Joe. But that was nothing compared to what was in front of us now. Mr. Gonzalez, Roland's dad, stood at the register paying for a couple of quarts of oil. He turned around and what was a glance became a glare. Danny went as pale as he had Friday night looking at the team photo in the Pizza Hut. Until right then, he'd never really had to look either of Roland's parents in the eye. He'd ditched the calling hours and the funeral. When they pressed criminal charges, he sat in court and kept his head down the whole time. If it weren't for Uncle Jack's attorney brother-in-law from Austin, Danny would've gladly been the scapegoat. Scapegoat wasn't the right word though. I mean, he was there—that night. He was part of it. It was Danny's idea to be there. It had to be his fault. That was what the police kept telling me.

For me, looking at Mr. and Mrs. Gonzalez in that courtroom, the anger and grief in their eyes made me sick for weeks and months 'til I lost track really. I sobbed on the stand when they asked me about the accident. Kept looking over at Danny, who wouldn't look my way as their lawyer drilled me. Demanded I recount the details.

"You understand you have to tell the truth, the whole truth and nothing but the truth. Can you do that, Michelle?" said the Gonzalezes' lawyer.

I just kept crying. Seeing the jury. The judge. Uncle Jack and Aunt Sara sitting behind Danny.

"I was reading the book," I kept repeating.

"After the book . . . ," said the Gonzalezes' lawyer.

Suddenly in Atkin's Autoparts I remembered fireworks. Like in my dream. Were there fireworks that night? What did I tell them—it was all so . . . dark. I could feel myself getting uneasy, so I started counting in my head and when I got to five the feeling of uneasy—of fireworks—was gone.

Mr. Atkin handed Mr. Gonzalez his change and made for a shelf to finish restocking.

Mr. Gonzalez limped toward Danny and me still standing on the rubber THANKS AGAIN mat at the front door. His right hand was drawn in tight from the stroke he had a few years earlier. It was some sight to see a man once so thick and handsome wither up to be so frail. Thought we might step to the side, act like it wasn't happening. But Danny didn't move.

"My wife said you were back," Mr. Gonzalez said, stopping not a foot from us.

Danny pinned his eyes to the floor. His face tensed, and his hands trembled.

"I guess you know what it's like to lose someone now," said Mr. Gonzalez, each word stitched with sharp jagged edges.

"Now?" my brother asked, his head raised as he sparred eye to eye with Mr. Gonzalez.

What was Danny thinking? *Was* he even thinking?

"You were his best friend," said Mr. Gonzalez. "Do you think you acted like his friend that night?"

Danny cracked his neck to the left. He wanted to run. Fast and hard and never stop. It was written all over him just like on graduation night when he vanished.

"Not once," said Mr. Gonzalez, "not once did you say you were sorry—show any remorse to me or my family."

Danny hardened, clenching his strong jaw.

Mr. Gonzalez moved in closer. His hate dousing Danny.

"I prayed to God every single night to not want you to die the way my son did." Mr. Gonzalez's voice began to shake. "He was a good boy. He meant *everything* to the people in this town. And you worthless—"

"Leave him alone," I said, half surprised that it had been my voice.

Mr. Gonzalez paused, but his eyes fixed on Danny. He wanted to rip his heart out. He wanted Danny to feel, not imagine, the pain that he'd carried in heavy buckets year after year, dragging up those steps to his beautiful ranch home with nothing whatsoever to brag about. Nothing in the world, with his house full of useless daughters. Roland was his only son, his only hope. Everyone's hope of one of their own as a quarterback in the NFL. Not a grave marker at Hamlem Cemetery before graduation.

After Roland died, and even before his stroke, Mr. Gonzalez wasn't the burly big-armed man who would've played college football had it not been for the color of his skin. He became a man who cried in restaurants and on courthouse steps. And right then, he had become a man who stood in an auto parts store and cried in front of me and my brother and Mr. Atkin restocking WD-40.

He walked past us, and we both stood frozen. The bell over the door jingled.

"You okay?" I asked.

"Let's just get the part and go."

We were a little ways past the Catholic church when Albert's black Chevy S10 pulled up. The tinted automatic windows rolled down.

"Hey," he said, stretching across the passenger side. "Where you two headed?"

I looked at Danny, who stared at the ground while taking a drag off his cigarette.

"The truck broke down off of Three Eights." I held up a small paper bag. "We had to walk in to get a part at Atkin's."

"Well, hop in," he said eagerly.

Again I looked at Danny.

"It's a long walk, come on," encouraged Albert.

Danny nodded for me to get in as he flicked his cigarette. I crunched into the middle, and we were on our way.

"How you been, Danny?" asked Albert.

Danny rolled the window down even though the air was full blast.

"Fine," he said, without any kind of feeling.

Albert smiled at me. "Were you over at Jack's?"

"Yeah," I said. "Sunday barbecue."

It seemed like years since Danny and I had been there. Not a couple of hours.

"You getting settled, Danny?" Albert said.

"Something like that," Danny said, lighting up another cigarette.

"I told Mickey you're more than welcome to come by the garage. Even bring in your father's truck if you want."

"Albert, I don't mean to be rude," Danny said, turning to him. "But this ain't a good time for catch-up."

Danny looked back out the window.

I took in a deep breath, wishing I were anywhere but in the middle of that tension sandwich.

"Okay," said Albert.

When we pulled up to the truck, Danny hopped out without so much as a thanks for the lift. I'd started to slide out when Albert said, "Mickey, do you need me to take you home?"

Danny looked at me.

"No, that's okay. It's an easy fix."

"You sure you don't need some help?" Albert said, tilting his head to Danny.

Danny shook his head as he closed the door behind me.

"Okay. See y'all later then."

Albert dropped the gearshift into drive, watching me out the passenger window as his truck rolled away. What was I thinking? Stay with Danny? And on Three Eights no less, where buzzards were the only thing that might come by on a Sunday afternoon.

Danny didn't so much as grunt from fixing the truck to the drive home. He must've smoked a half a pack of cigarettes though. I could almost see smoke oozing out of his greasy pores. When we got back to the house, it was dark and I made for my room while he milled about. TV on, TV off. Open the fridge, close it. Carefully, I stepped to my door and locked it, realizing right after that if he was really going to flip, that dinky lock wasn't gonna keep him back. It would be like tying a wounded tiger up to a tree with a piece of sewing thread. He picked up the phone and dialed. I could tell by the beeps that it was a long-distance call. Wisconsin? Arizona? Where would Danny call for help—for anything?

I squatted at the bottom of the door and heard, "Hi, it's me. Guess you're out. I just needed—I don't know. I feel like I'm . . ." And he paused real long. "I'll call you later. Don't call me back here."

The phone keypad beeped.

"Michelle," he hollered.

"Yeah," I answered, getting up real quick.

"There's ten bucks on the table. I'm going out."

The screen door banged open, slapping the outside of the house. I went to the window and watched him cut out the gate. He stopped in the driveway, gripping the back of the truck. Loosely rocking himself back and forth. He rolled his head back and forth in a real hard ironic "no," kicking the toe of his boot into the ground.

He turned and caught me watching, and there it was, that look from the photograph taken graduation night six years ago. It sent the hair straight up on my arms and my heart into my throat. He sprang his palms from the tailgate, leaving the truck behind. He didn't have his stuff, but maybe he didn't need it. Maybe that was what he did. Set up camp and then vanished and didn't take a thing with him.

He walked off down the street. I could taste the words in the back of my throat clawing their way to my dry tongue. My mouth opened wide enough for a heavy breath and that was all. In the dirty dim yellow streetlights, Danny's shape seemed simple, like an outline. Somewhere between the splashes of dull color, he disappeared.

I guess that was easy for a shadow to do.

12

The phone rang sometime around six Monday morning. Danny had been charged with disorderly conduct and resisting arrest. He had managed to get drunk and stay that way until he stumbled over to the twenty-four-hour Kwik 'N' Go sometime around five. He ran around playing invisible cowboys and Indians or some kind of stupid game with his finger pointed in the shape of a gun.

I couldn't find the keys to the truck, so I called Uncle Jack while I shoved a piece of bread into the toaster. I got dressed, gathered my books and was making for the door when I heard his horn honking.

"Morning," said Uncle Jack as I plopped into his car.

I snapped on my seat belt. "I can't believe this. Couldn't he just pass out in a field?"

"Two of you have words?" he asked, pulling out of the driveway.

"Nope."

"Seems kind of strange for him to just go off and get like that."

"Everything about him is strange," I said.

"You sure there wasn't something else going on? Could it have been the thing with Joe Sanchez yesterday?"

I pressed my forehead against the window, feeling my head vibrate on the glass.

"Mickey?"

"We ran into Roland's dad after we left your place."

"How did that go?"

"We're on our way to the police station, aren't we?"

I shifted in the pleather chair as Uncle Jack talked to Deputy Olivarez, Christina's second-oldest brother. Aside from a coat of putrid blue-green paint, the dinky police station hadn't changed much since that night six years ago. They had me in the sheriff's office until a little past two a.m. *What happened first? What did you see, Mickey? Can you tell us what you saw just as it was? Whose idea was the fire?*

"Where's Danny?" I kept asking. "I wanna see my brother."

Six years later and the last person I wanted to see that morning was Danny. I told myself that I could go on to school. There was nothing Uncle Jack couldn't take care of, but there I was feeling responsible. Like I could see Danny getting ready to crack last night, and I didn't— Uhh! All the noise in my head was making me nauseous.

Uncle Jack stepped away from the counter and sat beside me.

"They were waiting on the sheriff, but he's stuck just north of San Antonio. So they're going to let me post bail."

A deputy brought Danny out. He was dusty and had grass stains on both knees. The stench of beer and vomit caught air from a box floor fan in a matter of seconds.

Danny signed his name to get his plastic bag of belongings, including the lighter, his wallet and a damp cigarette. When we hit the parking lot, he threw his arm over my shoulder and said, "Thanks for showing up."

I shoved him away.

"You stink like Dad used to."

"Screw you, Mickey."

"Screw you, Danny, and don't call me that."

I got in the front seat of Uncle Jack's car. Danny stood there for a moment before Uncle Jack went over to talk to him. When Uncle Jack put his hand on Danny's shoulder, Danny jerked away and slammed into the backseat.

"Look, I'm sorry," said Danny, lighting up the cigarette.

"Yeah, no kidding."

Uncle Jack got in and buckled his seat belt.

"We all ready?" he asked.

Neither one of us said anything.

"Danny," said Uncle Jack, turning over the ignition. "Really appreciate it if you wouldn't smoke in the car, son."

Danny took a drag off his cigarette. A deep hard drag,

'cause I could hear the end of it crackle as if it were buried inside my eardrum. Then he rolled the window down and flick-spun it past the side of the car.

"Thanks," said Uncle Jack, easing away from the station.

"Drop him off first," I said.

"Ain't you late?" asked Danny.

Even though I was late for school, I didn't want anyone to see us pull up with him all hungover. That was for sure.

"Michelle, you are late," said Uncle Jack.

I didn't answer back.

He stopped the car at a four-way intersection, wrestling with what to do. Then he turned on his left blinker and headed away from the direction of the high school.

Danny was stinking up the whole car, so I rolled the window all the way down. Even then, it felt like I couldn't breathe, so I started counting in my head. I hit fifty-three just as we pulled up to the house.

"I'll come by on my lunch hour," Uncle Jack said to Danny.

"What for?" Danny asked.

"I think we need to talk," said Uncle Jack. "About how you're getting settled."

I looked in the rearview mirror and had a clear sight of Danny. He would probably be gone by lunch. If we were all lucky.

"You eat, Michelle?" Danny asked.

"Like you care."

He shook his head, kicked out of the backseat and jumped the back gate. When we pulled out of the driveway, I saw him sitting on the swing set pushing off as hard as he could. It looked like it was going to break.

I came in tardy to history just minutes before the end of class. Ricky cocked his head around and mouthed, "You okay?"

I nodded.

When the bell rang, I shot toward my locker. I looked up from the floor long enough to catch a cluster of big-haired girls watching me walk past. I figured it was all over school about Danny getting picked up, but that wasn't it at all. I followed where all their eyes shifted and there he was. That Kid, the one who caused Dad to swerve, he was back in school. I knew right off who he was from the newspaper picture printed next to Dad's the week before. He was getting books from his locker with this petite baby-faced girl standing beside him. That Kid, who didn't seem big enough to even be in high school, was the reason Dad died. No way did he have a clue what he'd done.

His friend saw me, and nudged him. Before he could turn around, I looked away.

I made it to lunch with a block of cement in my stomach and acid gurgling in my throat. I didn't even bother to go through the lunch line. Just grabbed a seat to wait for Christina. She had a Key Club meeting and was meeting me in the cafeteria afterward. It wouldn't have been a big deal except on her way out the door Mrs. Alvarado saw me sitting alone. She walked over with a grilled chicken salad and a slab of chocolate cake in hand.

"Hi, Michelle," she said, smiling. "How are you?"

Was she really doing this there? In the cafeteria where everyone could see and chew on it later?

"I'm good," I said, doodling in the margin of my book cover.

"I got a call from Sharon in the office. She said you were late this morning. You know, I'm really here to help you in any way you need."

"No. Everything's fine," I said.

"Are you eating? Can I get you something?"

"I'm *fine*." We both paused at my tone. "I'm just waiting."

She touched my shoulder and made my skin crawl. Crawl right off my body and into that cluckless grilled chicken in her salad.

"You let me know if you need anything. We all just want to help you through this."

Through what? I was already through.

"Hey, Mickey," said a voice.

I turned and saw Ricky strutting up with Johnny Lee.

"Mrs. A," Ricky said, holding a tray.

She smiled politely at them. "How are you?"

"No worries," said Ricky. "You know, me and Johnny Lee read every single book you have on the college list."

Johnny Lee nodded.

"Very impressive," she said, fake-smiling as always. Did that make her face hurt as much as mine did just from watching her? "Maybe a few less ditch days next year though. Attendance is part of graduation."

Ricky shrugged. "Yeah. I'll work on that."

"Well, I'll see you, Michelle," she said. "And let me know—"

"I will," I interrupted, and she walked away.

Ricky and Johnny Lee slid into a couple of seats across from me.

"Hope that wasn't important," Ricky said. "She kind of gets on my nerves with her pamphlets and handouts, you know."

I grinned. "Yeah, I know."

"Hey, brought you something." Ricky slid over a square cheese pizza on foil.

"I'm not really . . . hungry."

"Sure you are. Besides, Johnny Lee and me ran into Christina in the hall and she said to make sure you ate lunch. I mean, it's cool to have a girl faint at my feet but not because she needs to eat."

Was this guy for real? Nobody was this popular and nice *and* would give me the time of day. I was in a T-shirt with a chocolate milk stain, for Christ's sake. I nudged the pizza toward Johnny Lee.

"I already had three of them. Thanks, Michelle," he said, sliding it back my way.

"You feeling, um, better?" Ricky asked.

"Yup," I said, taking a huge bite out of the pizza.

"I thought maybe that was why you were late," he said. "That maybe you were sick."

"Nope."

"That's good, you know, 'cause—"

"Hey, Ricky, what's up?" I half turned to see Chuck Nelson and the Lettermans.

It was ninety freaking degrees outside and those idiots had on those stupid jackets. Their faces red and collars soaked in sweat. Except for Chuck. His jacket dangled in his hand like a straightedge.

"What's up, Chuck?" Ricky said, all nonchalant.

"Just hanging out." Chuck smirked at me before looking back at Ricky. "We're heading to the parking lot. Listen to Bobby's new system. Eight hundred dollars this guy dished out on it."

"I had to work my ass off for it," Bobby said.

"Begging your dad," Roy added.

Bobby slugged Roy in the shoulder. They were a scary bunch, those guys. Their size kept most of the students in check. But before they were big, they were just well-off and mean. They spent the good part of my freshman year passing around drawings of me with a hairy chest and chicken legs. All because the one kiss I ever had was with Chuck in sixth grade, and I screwed up and told my best friend at the time that he cried afterward. Before long, it was all over the elementary that tough guy Chuck cried when he kissed a girl. That he must be queer.

"Why don't you guys come with us?" Chuck said.

"We're cool," Ricky said.

"Right." Chuck got a couple of steps away and turned around. "So, Mickey, I almost forgot. How's your brother? Heard he was stumbling around last night drunk as hell. Good thing he wasn't driving, like your dad."

"Lay off it," Ricky said.

"No, no, get this, man. It gets better." Chuck came back

to the table, pressing his palms along the edge. "The guy really is crazy."

I inhaled a shaky breath. My whole body trembled. I started counting in my head but the numbers weren't loud enough. I think my mouth was moving with the numbers because of the way Johnny Lee watched me.

"We're at the Pizza Hut Friday night," said Chuck. "And Owens starts beatin' the shit out of the claw machine. Just goes apeshit."

Chuck imitated Danny shouting and beating on the machine in overexaggerated motions.

The Lettermans cackled. My skin felt warm. Hot. My face flushed red. Ricky saw it, and this time he didn't ignore it.

He stood up and threw his shoulders back. "Say you're sorry."

"What?"

Ricky held his stance. "Say you're sorry."

Chuck's expression sharpened into his game face. A face you didn't want to ever look at off the field. "I ain't apologizing to her. Everyone knows she's worthless white trash."

Johnny Lee kicked his seat back. The Lettermans were stunned.

"You guys are serious?" Chuck asked.

"He said apologize," said Johnny Lee, a little unsure.

Chuck laughed.

"Wow, the silent quarterback speaks. You remember, Miller, that arm is the only thing that stands between you and me. Don't push this. You don't wanna fight me over *that*." Chuck jerked his head toward me.

The lunchroom got so quiet that all I could hear was cupped-hand whispers and the jukebox playing Mariah Carey's "Emotions."

Mr. Thomas, the geometry teacher, jogged from his table and stepped between them. "What's going on here, boys?"

"Nothing," Ricky said, his eyes fixed on Chuck's. "Just talking about the off-season."

"Well, seems you'll have plenty of time to do that in seventh-period athletics. Come on, Chuck, Bobby. Let's all go back to lunch. Come on."

Mr. Thomas pushed the Lettermans along by their elbows.

Chuck leaned in so close I could smell raw onions and french fries steaming off his hot breath. "Maybe he'll just *play* with the matches this time."

I deflated to the back of my chair.

"I said leave her alone!" shouted Ricky.

Ricky shoved Chuck. Chuck shoved Ricky. Mr. Thomas got back between them as it was five on two with the Lettermans and Johnny Lee swinging, and right then Christina walked in with her jaw open as wide as the state of Texas itself. It came to me in a flash. Just like in honors English when I saw the jacket . . .

Roland was at the top of the bleachers. Why was he in the bleachers? That was it, he was . . . I had The Outsiders *flipped open:*

Easy, Ponyboy. . . .

I started counting again. One two three four five six . . .

Danny's head was buried under the truck seat, his hand feeling around for that lighter.

Johnny, I'm scared. . . .

Seven eight nine ten eleven twelve . . .

Roland shouted, "Hey, Mickey, check this out!"

I turned, laughing. . . .

I pushed away from the cafeteria table with my hand over my mouth, but it was too late. I threw up all over everything. Students gagged—scattered.

What was happening to me?

I splashed water on my face in the girls' bathroom. Christina held a cold wet paper towel on the back of my neck. Water dripped from the edges and rolled into a V, splatting against the sink.

"What's wrong with me?" I asked, my voice reverberating in the sink.

"Shhh. . . . Don't make yourself sick."

"I already did *that*. I feel like I'm . . ." I couldn't say it.

I couldn't begin to entertain the idea that I was losing it. That what everyone expected to happen was happening. That I was finally becoming just like Danny. Crazy.

I raised my head and felt a sweeping head rush and gripped the sink tightly for a moment.

"Just breathe, Gringa."

After a few breaths, I crouched up against the cool green brick wall and slid down to the floor.

"Do you think I'm . . . ?"

"What, not perfect?" Christina asked. "Mickey, your dad just died. That's—major."

"I can deal. I can get through."

"This isn't like a science test."

"What do you mean?" I said, hearing my stomach gurgle.

"I mean you can't just read chapter nine and learn the boldface print and ace the exam."

"I don't even know if I know the questions."

"Then don't worry so much about the answers," she said. "Just get through the rest of this month and get outta here. There's nobody in this world who wants that for you more than me. Except maybe Jesus, the saints and Jack, I guess."

She earned a half grin out of that.

"We wanna see you make it out of this town. I mean, I know *I* never will."

"Stop it," I said.

"You stop it."

She dropped her head, trying to shake the reality of her life off. "But you'll get out. No one's going to hold you back because of all this."

My eyes started to water up, so I buried my head in my knees. I wasn't gonna cry. I hadn't yet and I wasn't then. It didn't change anything. It didn't.

"I hate Danny," I said. "He ruins everything."

"So your stupid brother can't be everything you wanted him to be, so what? Hell, I got seven of those *pendejos*, and they're all duds but one. I know about wanting."

"It's not the same," I said. "You don't understand. You don't get it."

I got up and splashed more water on my face.

"What?" she asked. "Talk to me, Mickey. You don't have to hold it all in."

126

I rolled out a scratchy brown paper towel and dried my face.

"Nothing. I'm fine."

"Look, you wanna keep lying to me? I'm your best friend. You're not fine."

I grabbed my books.

"Don't be like this, Gringa."

"I'll catch you later."

I straightened my shoulders and headed out of the restroom. I could do it. I wasn't Ponyboy. I grew up. I could get through.

13

On the way back to class, I saw Ricky sitting outside the principal's office. I stood there for a moment watching him stare out the glass double doors leading to the front of the building. A subtle calmness and ease filled out his face, with his almost hypnotic gaze on the washed-out blue sky. His left eye was swollen with highlights of lavender and yellow. Against his complexion, it was like looking at a rare, beautiful budding flower.

"Hey," I said.

He snapped his head around to me. "Hey. You okay?"

"I'll never eat pizza on foil again before a school fight."

"It's cool," he said, grinning. "I ate five tacos during

football two-a-days one time freshman year and threw up all over the place."

"That's really gross."

"Yeah, kinda is, huh?"

"So," I said, stepping toward the glass doors. "You still waiting for the sky to fall?"

"Maybe. You?"

"I don't know," I said, changing the subject. "You and Johnny Lee gonna get in trouble?"

"Are you kidding? We play football. They'll bring Coach in, and he'll say he'll have us running until we puke up our guts."

"Will he?"

Ricky nodded, grinning real wide. "Yeah, probably. But it's cool. Besides, me and Johnny Lee have been a little iffy with Chuck since regionals. Chuck opened the line up on purpose and that's when Johnny Lee got hammered."

"Still. Johnny Lee seems kind of the nonfighter type."

"Oh yeah, totally, but he always backs me. Kinda like your brother and Roland."

Things suddenly got more than uncomfortable—

"Hey, I'm—sorry. I usually think before I . . . say things. I don't usually tell girls I threw up five tacos either."

"Then why me?" Thinking it was 'cause he saw me as one of the guys.

His cheeks puffed up for a few seconds before he blew air out the corner of his mouth. All the while, he ran his James Brown artificial tat hand through his hair.

"Just kinda want to. Not just tacos, I mean. Talk." He

tipped his head toward the principal's shut door, then back at me. "Listen, you wanna cut out of here? My car's by the stadium. I'll drive us out to the river. Or the city—"

"No. Not the city."

I couldn't imagine being on the highway Dad died on right then, if ever.

"Then you name it," said Ricky.

I had never ditched a class in my life. I prided myself on perfect attendance. It made me feel consistent, dependable and, most of all, stable. None of that came to mind as we crept down the hallways and slunk past classroom windows on our way to the football stadium.

When we got into his car, Ricky snapped on his seat belt as a wave of anxiousness crashed into me. I sat there, sweat dripping down the back of my neck, with the belt pulled halfway across my chest, completely frozen.

"Mickey? Sure this is cool?" he said, his left hand resting on the wheel. "We can still go back. I mean . . . it's cool."

I wasn't sure about anything anymore except that being with Ricky made more sense than anything had in the last week. How crazy was that?

"No," I said, snapping my seat belt buckle. "Besides. Like you said, you don't live forever, right?"

Nodding, he grinned. "Right."

He turned over the ignition and slid the gearshift into reverse. Rolling the wheel with one hand, he slipped in a CD with the other.

When his car cut the edge of the parking lot, I dropped the seat back and stared out the window. Everything about ditching with him was wrong, but I didn't care. I didn't care about being right—doing right. Not then. 'Cause I just felt free watching everything pass, like we weren't driving but floating. Floating right up into the sky.

Riding out to The Stick with Ricky was different than any other time I had been out there. I'd never been there with anyone but Danny. Soon as we turned down that slim road, I pushed the seat back up. Hedges of dust burst behind his clunky car, coughing and rattling most of the way. Just one deep enough pothole, I thought, and the whole car might fall into hundreds of pieces all at once.

He wedged the car onto the skinniest strip of the road before stopping where it was only wide enough for two people to walk. Sweat ran down under my arms and along my sides. I really wished I'd put on deodorant that morning.

I shoved the door open, and it screamed.

"Maybe some grease on the hinges," he said, climbing out the window.

"Maybe?"

I sat on the hood, watching him skip rocks down the road.

"You come out here a lot?" he asked.

"Not anymore. Why?"

"I like it. It's . . . quiet," he said. "I like quiet."

"Right."

"Why would I lie?" he asked, flinging a rock.

"Why wouldn't you?"

"Because it's boring."

The softness in his smile put my every nerve on end. No one could think The Stick was cool except my crazy brother.

"Danny useta say that you could see the whole world, or at least ten miles in either direction, from this spot," I said. "That you could always see what was coming. Even the fields were tattletales in the way they moved. If somebody tried to sneak up on you, those stalks would go to talking and swaying. Except with Danny. It was kinda like he moved through them, never between them. Like a ghost."

"Tough break," Ricky said.

"What?"

"Your brother." He flung another rock. "It's gotta be hard. Living with something like what happened. And to come back here . . ."

"Yeah, I guess."

"Hey, I'm not defending him. I just think . . ." He wheeled a rock out. "It's a tough break. I mean, if it had been the same, only with me and Johnny Lee. I don't know what I would do. Probably jump right off the Harbor Bridge."

His eyes followed another rock dropping way down the road.

"I guess Danny can't find a high enough bridge," I said. "Either that or he's just crazy."

He chunked a clod of dirt.

"You really think your brother's crazy?" he asked.

I hadn't really considered it that way. Not so point-blank. I mean, I'd said it I don't know how many times in my head—but was he? Was he really nuts?

"Sure. Why not?" I said.

"Maybe," Ricky said. "I mean, I don't know a lotta crazy people. Or maybe he just, I don't know, can't deal. At least he's not doing what a lotta guys who played football that year are doing."

"What do you mean?"

"Slinging burgers, bagging groceries. Buying new trucks when their family's on welfare. Those guys come up to Johnny Lee and me bragging about how they rushed for ten or fifteen yards at state. But it's like, look at them now. Wishing they had done things . . . different. I mean, they don't say it, but you can . . . see it."

"And you're gonna be different?" I asked.

"I'm already different. Aren't you?"

He picked up another clump of dirt and flung it wildly in the air. It burst apart and showered down.

"What?" he asked.

"Why do you ditch all the time?" I said.

"I get bored."

"That's no reason to ditch," I said. "Everyone gets bored. It's high school. The whole idea of it is smothering."

"Exactly, that's what I mean. That's what I like about you—you get that." He sat down on the hood. "I just have to come up for air. It's like Johnny Lee always says. How he can't stand all that rah-rah stuff. I mean, I love football, sometimes I think more than Johnny Lee, but all that crap. It just gets so . . . you know?"

He waited for me to say something, but I never did well on the spot.

"Besides, just because I ditch sometimes doesn't mean I'm stupid," he said. "I mean . . . I'm not stupid."

"Why do you keep saying that?"

"Because I know . . . I'm good at football, skateboarding

and hopefully fixing up this car. But a lot of people still see me as the dumb kid who flunked kindergarten."

"I don't think you have to worry especially, 'cause you have the popularity contest won."

"Like I said, that's all rah-rah. That stuff's smoke . . . and mirrors. I mean, when I go to college none of that's gonna matter. Anyway . . . I just didn't want you to think I was dumb. I mean, I get how smart you are." He turned his head toward me. "I think that's real cool. That you're not afraid to be you."

"You're not afraid to be you," I said.

He shyly grinned, pressing his finger to his lips. "Shhh . . . I'm scared of a lotta things. Don't tell anyone. But getting out of Three Rivers isn't one of them. That's for sure. And . . . you don't seem scared of that either."

I'd never looked into a guy's eyes and felt so completely seen before. Like he was scrolling through every memory I had and deciding whether or not to keep them for his own. I wanted to give them to him and somehow wanted to run screaming from him at the same time.

"Can I ask you something?" I said.

He nodded.

"What did you see? When you looked up every day at recess in kindergarten?"

His lips held together as his cheeks rose. "The sky. I saw the sky up there." He threw his head back. "My grandmother, she was two halves: religion and storytelling. She useta tell me how the sky would fall if you didn't watch it close enough. That just in these parts, these pieces, it would crumble down until it was nothing. And only if you looked

134

faithfully with your heart so open could you really see it. And seeing meant saving."

Ricky made the sky sound fresh as spring grass. The glint of sunlight in his green eyes as he talked was evidence of something more beautiful than anything I'd ever imagined all on my own. He did see something up there that no one else did. For a second, I saw something too.

"Of course," he said, "it made my mother really pissed because I'd come home with these teacher conference slips. She knew I wasn't dumb but they all thought I belonged in special ed, you know. 'Behavioral disorder—learning disorder.' Didn't matter that I could read and write at a second-grade level in kindergarten, you know. But . . . my grandmother—she somehow"—and his whole face lit up like she was standing right beside him—"talked my mom into keeping me out of special ed. So they held me back a year. That repeat year, my grandmother said on the first day of school, 'The sky will wait for you, *mijo*. Do what they tell you.' And I did. Well, for the most part."

Ricky let his face, his shoulders, his whole body express one feeling to the next. How he did that and still got to hang in the A-crowd blew my mind in half a dozen different directions. Maybe he didn't show them that part.

"After my grandmother died," he said, "I guess I kept looking. Not thinking I kept the sky from falling, but, I don't know . . . how it kept me from falling. Mrs. Alvarado's pamphlets didn't exactly do the trick, you know?"

I smiled.

"Besides, it's still up there. Clouds drifting by from here to Mexico to China to somewhere." A swooping breeze blew his thick hair across his face. "I'm really sorry, Mickey. That I don't know really what to say about your dad."

"You don't have to say sorry," I said.

"No, but I want to. I'm really glad we came out here. I mean, it's kind of cool to finally just talk." His voice cracked on the last word. "I always wanted to talk to you."

"Right," I said, laughing. "Guys don't want to talk to me unless they need tutoring."

"I told you. I'm not dumb."

Ricky leaned on the hood about a foot away from me. I never realized how short a foot was until Ricky Martinez hung over me. There was something so . . . real about him. No games. No showing off. He was the lead in every great cable teen show that we never got at home but I heard about in first period. Ricky was the good guy. I was dizzy.

"Mickey," he said, clearing his throat.

"Yeah . . . ?" My heart raced, and I mean twenty-feet-from-the-finish-line raced.

"You think I could kiss you?"

The answer was obvious. Obviously *Yes! Kiss me!* Aside from that awful sixth-grade kiss with Chuck, no one but my dad had ever kissed me and that was gross after fourth grade. The answer had been obvious since kindergarten when Ricky grinned at me in the lunch line. So I couldn't believe as he leaned in that I dropped my head away.

"Sorry," he said, defeated. "That was way uncool."

I was so embarrassed and confused and nauseous all at the same time. The thought of hurling again was more than I could bear.

He slid through the driver's window and sat in the car.

I stretched back on the hood with my head against the windshield.

I looked to the east. The clouds swelled bubbly angry pink and flat-bottomed. The fallen veins of lightning ignited, burned out. Sizzled, settled. All across the sky, stretches of powder-black clouds dumped sheets of rain some twenty or so miles away. You could smell it in the air. The way the eighty-degree heat briskly turned cooler and fell sick like a cold sweat. You could feel it chase up under your T-shirt sleeve and linger at your neck.

You could feel the storm that was coming.

The traffic lights swung wildly. The school zone blinkers had stopped flashing and anyone who could be inside was. Big gusts of wind wailed against Ricky's car and squeezed out a faint holler across its feeble frame. We hadn't said a word to each other all the way back. The notion of a kiss being part of whatever came next seemed everything right and everything wrong.

He cut the corner to my block and the wind shook us a little too hard. We swerved onto the wrong side of the road for just a second.

"Sorry," he said softly.

His grip on the wheel finally loosened as he pulled up outside my house.

"Thanks," I said.

"For what?" he asked.

Before I could get out another word, Danny exploded, and I mean exploded, out the screen door. Ricky's eyes fell right toward Danny charging at us. I popped the handle and stepped out into the wind blowing everything on me backward. Ricky turned off the engine and was halfway out when Danny yelled, "Don't do it, man," flexing his index finger at him.

"Calm down," I said.

Danny's eyes didn't leave Ricky. "Get in the car, man, and drive away."

"Quit it, Danny," I yelled.

He squeezed my arm. "What are you doing? The school called. The police came by."

"Everyone ditches," I argued.

"No, everyone does not, and according to Mrs. Alvarado, queen of guidance, you especially don't—"

"Mr. Owens," Ricky interrupted.

"Kid, get in the car. Get in!" A cloud of black swelled in Danny's eyes.

Ricky reluctantly eased back inside, eyeing me once more before he turned his car back on and hesitantly drove off.

I flung my arm away from Danny's tight grip. "Why do you do this?"

"What? Care what happens to you?" Danny asked.

"You really are crazy," I said.

The wind roared and the neighbor's wind chimes smashing together was the only sound aside from cracking leaves that pierced the smothering air. Danny threw his hands up and ran them through his greasy hair. I ran toward the house with his voice trailing, swallowed in the gust.

I yanked my jumbo duffel from under my bed. Dug through drawers and grabbed only the necessities. The wind howled and coiled its heavy hollow body, sweeping the outside of the house again and again. Dad would've understood. Dad would've never grabbed me like that, like a stupid doll with plastic eyes and plastic arms. Dad would've—Danny busted into my room, a locomotive out of control.

"Get out, Danny."

"What are you doing?"

"Leaving," I snapped.

He reached around me and unpacked my bag, and I repacked and before I knew it we were tug-of-warring my favorite T-shirt.

"Cut it out, Danny."

"We're gonna talk. We're gonna try," he said.

And then the shirt ripped clear up the side and he kind of let out a laugh and that was it. I shoved him, and he fell right up against the dresser drawers. I stood there dangling my rag of a shirt like a Spanish matador waving a red cape. It didn't take much to imagine him a bull, with the look on his face.

"I don't get you," he said, pushing himself up from the dresser. "You got all this stuff going for you. Special school and you what? Ditch with some punk—"

"Shut up and get out," I yelled, gathering up my stuff.

"You wanna end up like me?" he said. "Do you?"

I spun around and charged right up in his face. "No! The last thing I want to be is anything that's like you. The day you ran off was the best day of my life. At least I didn't have to hear you go off on Dad all the time about how he just couldn't be enough for you. So don't give me the big brother 'I care about you' crap. If you cared, you'd finally grow up. I did."

I didn't flinch or work up one tear the whole time I unloaded on him.

Glaring at me, he reached into his back pocket and held out *The Outsiders*. "Well, if you're moving, you probably want to take this with you."

I stood there so angry that a low shake rampantly roared through my whole body. Every capillary—every nerve ending—tensed and rose to the surface, pulsating. The thunder shook the whole house and the leaves sounded like wood crackling on a campfire.

I grabbed that stupid book out of his hand and split it, and I mean split it right down the middle.

"Grow up," I said.

His glare faded into defeat, into something small but big. I shoved the last of my stuff that could fit into the bag and zipped it up as much as I could.

"You ain't Darry and I ain't Ponyboy. This ain't *The Outsiders*," I said, flinging my bulging bag over my shoulder. "And there are no happy endings."

I snatched up my backpack from the corner and split.

He wasn't getting another minute out of me. Not a single one. I hit the yard, flung open the gate and when the sky lit up and the ground shook I didn't feel a thing. I looked up as pieces of hail dropped and knew it was just going to fall. The whole damn sky.

14

Uncle Jack's soothing *Father Knows Best* voice carried from the kitchen into the bathroom. He was on the phone with Danny, who'd called the minute we walked in, wanting to talk to me. Fat chance, psycho.

I peeled out of my wet clothes and hung them over the shower rod. I'd stood outside the Aycock Gas and Go for something like ten minutes before Uncle Jack pulled up. Ten minutes of the guy at the counter watching me get sprayed with rain and pelted by hail as I nestled up next to the phone booth. I must've looked crazy. Crazy to stand outside in green-sky tornado weather. But to go inside where he and a couple of customers were riding out the storm, no way. There would be questions. There would be looks. Looks worse than "what's that crazy Owens girl doing standing in the rain?" At least I'd somehow worked it out in my mind that way.

I wrapped a towel around me and squatted down to unzip my drenched duffel. I picked the really soaked clothes off the top and bottom and flung as many of them as I could over the shower rod and towel holders. Somehow a pair of jeans and a gray T-shirt with the GIVING BLOOD IS LOVE logo sprawled across the chest had managed to stay dry. Dressed, I reached for the doorknob when all at once I felt so—I put my hands over my face and tried to . . . It wasn't cold, but I couldn't stop shivering. My teeth chattered. My fingers felt numb. Is that what it felt like in Roland's skin—is that—**what it was like inside a burning ember . . . ?**

The phrase startled me. Startled me 'cause it felt like my own, only it wasn't. Why was I thinking about something Ponyboy thought in *The Outsiders*? That stupid book had collected dust from nightstand to bookshelf for years. But there was that phrase trying to burrow its way in even deeper. Still shivering, I crossed my arms over my chest. I closed my eyes, breathing deep and slow, and by the time I counted to ten, I'd shaken it off.

Uncle Jack was still on the phone with Danny when I came out of the bathroom. Only now the microwave was on, so his voice melded with the hum of whatever he had cooking. I dropped my duffel at the foot of the stairs and walked over to the living room window and pulled back the curtain. The worst of the storm had tapered off into thin streaks of drizzle and left loose branches and turned-over lawn chairs scattered all over Uncle Jack's front yard. I slipped my damp frizzy hair behind my ears and plopped on the sofa, curling my legs up under me. Across the room, the clipping on the mantel of Danny and Roland stared at me. They were so stupid. No way was I going to blow it like them. I was careful and smart and in control. And most of all now, no way would Uncle Jack send me back to my nut-job brother.

The bowl of fortune cookie thoughts on the coffee table caught my eye. I reached in and unfolded one of the slips and it said: YOU WILL BE ONE OF THOSE PEOPLE WHO GOES PLACES IN LIFE.

Danny had read that same phrase when we came for the cookout on Sunday. Had Aunt Sara written it more than once? That wasn't like her. My hand hovered over the bowl when the microwave beeped and Uncle Jack stepped in the doorway, snapping the cordless phone on the charger. His eyes immediately fell to my hand holding the slip of paper.

"I was—just curious," I said, refolding it quickly. "Don't you ever wanna look?"

"Just put it back in the bowl, okay?" said Uncle Jack, each word lined with hurt.

"Okay."

Stupid, stupid, stupid. I knew better. It was an unspoken rule not to touch anything that had been Aunt Sara's. There I was fishing around that bowl without so much as a thought for Uncle Jack's feelings. Acting exactly like Danny.

"I'm sorry," I said.

"I made you something. Come on."

I rolled off the sofa and followed him into the kitchen.

I pulled out a chair at the table as Uncle Jack set a bowl of steaming mac 'n' cheese in front of me.

"Thanks," I said.

He eased into a chair beside me. "You ready to talk yet?"

"It's no different than what I said in the car." I blew on the macaroni. "I can't stay there. I don't care what he told you on the phone. I can't. You know that."

"Or is it that you won't?"

My hands trembled something awful. I didn't realize how long it had been since I'd eaten. Throwing up lunch and all.

"Mickey?"

"He ain't right." I blew harder on the mac 'n' cheese. "You should've seen him go off in front of Ricky."

"He was worried," Uncle Jack said. "You left school without permission. No one knew where you were—"

"He was crazy. 'Bout squeezed the feeling out of my arm. Ripped my favorite shirt."

I wolfed the mac 'n' cheese and burnt the heck out of the roof of my mouth.

"Slow down," he said. "Slow . . . down."

I dropped my fork into the bowl.

"There isn't anything legal around this, right?" I asked. "I mean, he can't keep me."

"Technically he *is* your family."

"You're my family more than he is," I said. "Uncle Jack? Dad had a will, right?"

"He had a will."

"And . . ."

"And he wanted you to be with me," Uncle Jack said, folding his fingers together. "But it's not about who you live with, Mickey."

"Sure is for me."

I picked my fork back up and stabbed up a stack of macaroni.

"Darlin', I'm the last one to defend your brother—"

I shook my head. "That's all everyone's been doing since he came back. You—Christina—Ricky. Just 'cause a person shows up doesn't make everything all right."

"No, it doesn't," said Uncle Jack. "Can you try and imagine how difficult this is for him?"

I clanged the fork against the bowl.

"You see. That's it," I snapped. "What's *difficult* for Danny. Poor Danny. Can't pull it together. I was there that night too."

"Yes?"

A sudden rush of heat splashed over me. I pushed the bowl away and slouched back into the chair. Uncle Jack sat silent, waiting. Waiting for me to say something as the thick quiet settled in. The only sound piercing it was the dripping of my clothes from the shower rod onto the edge of the tub. A sound that I never thought could be so loud. So lonely . . .

"You don't want me here anymore," I said.

"Mickey—"

"Is that what you're telling me? You don't want me, Uncle Jack?"

Uncle Jack inhaled a breath that swelled his chest out real big.

"You know better than that, but it's not that simple."

"This all sucks. All of it."

"All of what?"

"I want everything to be like it was before. Before Dad died and Danny went crazy and Mom ran away. Even if—"

145

I stopped myself.

"Even if what?" he asked.

I crossed my arms over my chest and shook my head. It didn't matter.

"Even if what, Mickey?"

"Nothing."

He took in a deep breath and rested his elbows on the table.

"You know, your father, he was my best friend growing up. The best kind of friend ever, and you've always been family to me."

"I know, I know—"

"No, now listen. But in spite of everything that went on between your brother and him, Danny didn't hesitate when I called. He took the first bus here."

"Well, give him a gold star for effort," I said. "But save me the After School Special about how big brother comes back and saves his parentless sister. I ain't playing the part." I leaned forward, feeling the anger rise clear up to the roof of my burnt mouth. "After all this time, he still has to get even with him."

"With who?" asked Uncle Jack.

"Dad," I said, figuring the answer had to be obvious. "He never forgave him for not going after Mom. He's just here to remind everyone how Dad screwed him up. He doesn't care who he spills it on."

Uncle Jack dropped his head and shook it.

"Mickey, I love you," he said, raising his eyes to me. "But if you don't know better than that, then you're not half as smart as I give you credit for being."

Before I was halfway out of my chair, Uncle Jack said, "Sit down and listen. This is the part where you get to exercise those grown-up muscles you think you've developed."

I huffed and sat back in the chair.

"That boy came back here, to the one place he never wanted to come back to, for you. You can shake your head and stomp your feet all you want, but the truth is he loves you."

"I don't need it," I said. "I don't need it anymore. I'm sorry, Uncle Jack. That's just how things are."

"That's fine," he said. "But know there's a lot more to growing up than getting out of this town. It's about facing the things that scare you."

"I ain't afraid." I held my eyes steadfast on his.

"All right, darlin'." He slid the bowl back toward me. "Eat this while I make some real dinner."

Uncle Jack wasn't the enemy, and I knew it. Still, there I had been all puffed up and fighting against him. It was a lousy way to be to the one person I could always count on. Really count on.

While he went from pantry to fridge, he struggled to straighten the slouch in his stance. He was worn out in a way I'd never noticed before. I couldn't stop looking . . . realizing—

"What are you thinking about?" he asked, slicing mushrooms on the cutting board.

Right then, the expression came to me as if automatic. With the stretch of my lips into a smile, just like all those laminated posters on Mrs. Alvarado's wall, I lied. And now I felt it. Felt deep in my gut why people did that and everything inside of me cringed that I was doing it.

"Nothing," I said, turning my attention back to the mac 'n' cheese.

He smiled in that comforting way that I knew really wasn't real. How could I've done that? My face hurt.

There wasn't one spot in the bed that felt easy that night. I tried reading, counting numbers in my head. Nothing could settle me. Every inch of muscle was tense. After two hours of restlessness, I lunged out of bed craving leftover tuna casserole. When I came out of my room, I saw Uncle Jack's door down the hall ajar. No light on.

I hung over the top of the banister as a dull spill of light crawled up the bottom step. I quietly went downstairs and stopped with my hand on the railing when I saw Uncle Jack sitting at the kitchen table crying. I stood there watching this man who had picked me up from scraped knees and bad dreams sit alone with Aunt Sara's yellow coffee mug between his hands and sob right out loud.

I scrunched up on the third stair from the bottom, some part of me thinking I should go and sit with him. The other part not knowing really how. I stayed there until he got up to go to bed. Then I slipped back into my room trying to imagine that I hadn't seen any of it, but knowing that I had.

15

I spent first period sitting in Mrs. Alvarado's office with Uncle Jack. Listening to the two of them talk back and forth about what was in my best interest. The welfare-of-the-child kind of talk I had heard more than once after Danny got into trouble.

Now there was the issue of the ditching and the fight in the cafeteria. There was the instability of my home and should the school intervene. My big brain had managed to buy me a ticket of "extreme concern" with my teachers and especially Mrs. Alvarado. The same people who championed my brother for college and then abandoned him after Roland died were now worried about me.

"Well, I don't see any reason for this to be a legal matter

if Danny won't contest Michelle's staying with you," said Mrs. Alvarado. "She'll be eighteen in August and well on her way to college. I don't think it's really an issue from the school's standpoint."

I wasn't sure what they were deciding or why I was nodding or why everything in her office was laughing out loud at me and I was the only one who could hear it.

"Michelle, there are probably a lot of questions—emotions that you're having. With your father and this trouble with your brother." The corners of her mouth went as high as they could without trembling. "What would be most helpful to you right now?"

I shrugged. "To go to second period."

Uncle Jack patted me on the knee. "Well, you better get on there, then. Thank you, Mrs. Alvarado." He held out his hand. "I'm sure everything will be all right."

"Michelle, you know—"

I looked at the door and then back at her. "It's always open. Got it."

Suddenly it felt like I'd held my breath the whole time we were in there. I exhaled the heaviest breath the minute we got out the door.

"Are you sure you're okay?" asked Uncle Jack. "No one is going to think any different of you if you stay home a few days."

"No. It's only a couple more weeks. That's all I gotta get through, right?"

"Right."

We walked toward the school as the second-period bell rang. Doors fanned open, almost synchronized. Everybody poured out, chattering, laughter swimming.

"I'll pick you up at three-thirty," he said, breaking toward the parking lot.

"Uncle Jack."

"Yeah?"

"Thanks."

He held up his hand in a gentle loving way that was a promise that things would be fine and that he would actually be there at three-thirty. He would stick.

I hurried along the breezeway and jogged to my locker, where Christina was already perched.

"Where have you been?" she demanded. "I called your house last night and your brother said you don't live there anymore."

"That's right," I said, unloading my books from my backpack.

"Well? What's going on?"

"Nothing," I said.

"Are you back at Jack's? Don't just stand there and ignore me, Mickey. What's going on?"

"Nothing!" I snapped.

She took a step back with her hands up. In all the years we'd hung out, I'd never kept anything from her. Not really, not until that last week. I couldn't look her straight in the eye, so I fidgeted with my locker handle.

A finger tapped me on the shoulder, and I spun around to see Ricky. I turned back to Christina.

"Maybe I'll see you later, Gringa." Christina stepped into the flow of students.

"Did I do something?" he asked.

"Nope," I said, jamming a spiral into my backpack.

"So, did your brother cool off?"

"Why? Do you wanna tell everybody what happened?"

"No . . . I was just worried."

"Right," I said, shutting my locker.

"What did I do? I'm—sorry I tried to kiss you."

"You know what, Ricky? Things are a little more complicated than something that stupid. See, for the rest of us mor-
tals, the coach doesn't step in and take care of things. For the
rest of us, what we do, it has a consequence. It's not about
crazy grandmothers and mystical stories about the sky."

He dropped his shoulder against the locker next to mine.

"What's wrong?" he asked. "I'm being real with you."

"Real? Right, you're being real."

"I am."

"Your family is one of the wealthiest in town, yet you
drive the junkiest car. You get to be tardy and ditch 'cause
you can make touchdowns. You'll go to a really good college
'cause of football or because you'll get some doe-eyed junior
to help you do your entrance essay. It's all cake. No effort.
And you know what, at the end of the summer I'm gone, so
what do you care anyway?"

"Hey, I am not a dumb jock, Mickey. And that story
about my grandmother, I *never* told that to anyone else. Not
even Johnny Lee."

"Yeah well, you shouldn't have wasted it on me."

I cleared the combination off my lock and cut through
the crowd for the doors at the end of the hall, not sure by a
mile, not even a mile and three-quarters, why I'd just treated
him like the worst guy I'd ever met.

Maybe he was.

During English Christina traded seats with Carla Jimenez and sat as far back and away from me as she could. It bothered me the way Christina's shoulders hung forward. Her arms crossed over her chest like she was protecting her heart.

In the cafeteria, I went through the lunch line and saw Christina not only sitting alone but not at our table. I carried my pink plastic tray with slops of rehydrated mashed potatoes and steak fingers toward her. Her nose was buried midway through *The Iliad* when I got there. I knew she knew I was standing there, but she flipped the corner of the page like I wasn't.

"Anyone sitting here?" I asked, trying to break the tension.

She didn't look up from her book. "It's empty, isn't it?"

I pulled out the seat across from her and popped the top of my Coke. Chuck Nelson with his shiner shining glared at me from the lunch line.

"People might think you're showing off reading that kind of book all out in the open," I said.

"People think a lot of things, Gringa. You can't stop them from their thoughts," she said, still reading. "For example, I *thought* we were friends, but it seems you think that only when it works for you."

"You're not going to hold a grudge 'cause I'm having a bad day."

"Mickey," she said, "even before your dad died most of your days were bad. They were just easier to ignore."

I'd never felt so small in my life.

"I'm sorry," I said.

153

"What? You might wanna speak up," she said. "See, I can't hear you over your ego."

"I said I'm sorry," I repeated, humbled.

"You know what you are, Mickey?" She laid the book facedown on the table. "You're selfish. You think that you have to do it all alone. 'No one can understand me 'cause I got abandoned.' You think all of a sudden I can't see what's going on with you? So I didn't live here six years ago when it all happened, but that don't mean I haven't listened." She shook her head and went back to her book. "You must think I'm one dumb stuck Mexican."

There wasn't much worse than Christina ignoring me. When you were off her radar, you were off.

"Forget this," she said. The feet of her chair squealed as she pushed away from the table.

"I said I was sorry."

"Look at me and tell me you mean it."

My eyes dropped to my tray. I couldn't lie to her. Not about anything real.

"Later, Gringa."

There was a difference between feeling alone and being alone. A difference I got smacked in the chest with right there.

After school, I climbed into Uncle Jack's car and heaved a huge sigh of relief that the day was finally over. That I wouldn't have to look at Christina blazing away from her locker to avoid me, or even think I might bump into Ricky again.

"Good day?" Uncle Jack said.

I nodded.

As we drove by the football field, Ricky and Johnny Lee

were off in the distance pulling old tractor tires with the coach fast on their heels. I imagined the phrases Coach shouted with those ropes digging into their shoulders. He seemed to reserve terms of endearment such as *maggot, faggot, loser, pansy* and *moron* for the ones he really liked. I had heard them all sitting in the stands watching Danny practice for hours and hours. He had a determination and love for football as expansive as the Texas sky itself. Nothing Coach shouted while dragging him by the face mask fazed him because the game flowed through Danny's veins richer and thicker than blood.

He was going to be famous.

Uncle Jack eased his car into the driveway. Danny's arms stretched along the front porch swing, gliding back and forth.

"What's he doing here?" I barked.

"Come on."

We got out of the car. I emptied the mailbox and headed up the steps behind Uncle Jack. The two of them shook hands like old war buddies.

"I just wanted to talk to Michelle for a moment," Danny said. "If that would be all right?"

Uncle Jack turned around and looked at me. "She's a big girl. She can decide that."

Reluctantly I nodded. Uncle Jack took the mail and disappeared inside the house.

"You leaving?" I asked.

He let the air stay quiet between us for long enough to be too long. "I wanna apologize. I was . . . I had every intention of doing right by you this time."

He swung up hard, jangling the swing chains, and I flinched enough to make us both uncomfortable.

"Mickey, Michelle. I never once raised a hand to you, even when we were kids. A lot of big brothers hated their little sisters. Treated them like punching bags. I never hurt you. Why are you so afraid of me?"

"You're so stupid," I said.

"Why?" he asked.

"I don't know why. You just are."

I leaned against the screen-door frame with my hand firm on the handle.

Danny reached for his inside jacket pocket and pulled out *The Outsiders*. He'd fixed the binding crooked with clear mailing tape.

"You're right," he said, shuffling the pages with his thumb. "I ain't Darry or Dally. Soda or Two-Bit. But I am your brother, and I will always be your brother."

I clamped my teeth together as hard as they'd go and pinned my eyes to the porch floor. No way was I gonna look soft the way I did in that college mirror.

"I done some things, Michelle. Bad things—stupid things. Mostly out of . . . I don't know. Out of trying to fill in this blackness inside of me, hoping it could be some kind of gold. But you gotta know. Leaving you behind—I regret it. I regret not knowing how to do it different." He held out the book to me. "Please. I fixed it for you," he said, every word struggling to make itself.

"Uncle Jack said your showing up here, it was for me," I said.

Danny nodded.

"Well, maybe you could leave for that reason too."

156

I don't know what Danny saw in my face, but it didn't take him long to quit looking. He got halfway down the porch steps before he stopped. He squeezed *The Outsiders* in his hand, bending its body into a U. Then he walked back up the steps and rested the book on the arm of the swing. He didn't look at me for a response, for anything.

He tromped down the steps, got into the truck and was gone.

16

The next day Christina ignored me through second period and didn't even show up to lunch. She had to be really pissed at me to miss hamburgers. It was one of the few meals she actually liked from the cafeteria.

I sat there trying to look interested in my brochure for the University of Dallas, a private school that had given me early admittance and a near-full scholarship. The day I got the acceptance letter in early March, Dad beamed. I hadn't seen him that happy since—since I don't know when really. Maybe never. Could he have never beamed until right then? He'd been dead over a week now. A week and somehow moments were already feeling vague—distant. Had they felt that way before? Did I somehow not notice?

I missed talking to Christina already. I—

"Is it all right with you if I sit?"

I raised my head and saw Johnny Lee standing with his tray across from me. His face was busted up pretty good from the fight with Chuck and the Lettermans. Just looking at him made me kind of wince.

"I don't have to," he said.

"No—I mean, yeah, sit," I said, surprised that he really wanted to.

Unbelievable. He slid out a chair. Aside from the last week, we had sat at the same table maybe twice since elementary—one time for sure in junior high and that was during a tornado warning. But there he was, the town superstar, situating his mustard and mayo, peeling back the bun of his burger across from me. He didn't seem like a superstar though. Sure didn't carry himself like the god the town needed him to be.

"What?" he said, startling me out of my stare.

I shrugged and awkwardly looked down at my tray.

"So, I guess if you're sitting here alone, you and Christina aren't talking?"

"Does everyone know my business?"

He shook his head. "Ricky and I stopped by the restaurant last night. He was worried about you. She seemed a little . . ."

"Like she hated me."

He half laughed. "Best friends don't hate each other. Besides, I don't think *most* people know what hate really means."

I stared down at my cold fries.

"I know what it means."

He rested his arms on the table. The moment of him

159

looking at me and me feeling like I'd just revealed what a cold heart I really had made me uneasy. I didn't even know him and I'd said it. Right out loud.

"Yeah, well," he said. "Maybe you're not like most people. I'm thinking you probably see things at a different slant."

"Why would you say something like that?"

"Well, we are in a lot of the same classes," he said, stating the obvious.

"Right . . ." I sipped my Coke.

He reached around and slapped a paperback all curled up from his back pocket onto the table.

"*Drown*?" I said, reading the binding.

"Ricky loaned it to me. His sister Olivia sent it to him from college. He really got into it. It's pretty good. If you like short stories."

"Where is Ricky?" I said, taking a bite of my burger.

Johnny Lee gave me that look. The look that said Ricky ditched and let's not go into it.

"I didn't get a chance to say thanks."

"What do you mean?" he said.

"For yesterday. I'm sorry about your face. Does it hurt? Okay, *that* was a dumb question."

"Yeah, it hurts. But only if I do something really insignificant like breathe."

His soft grin fell off quick as his brow furrowed. "Besides, Chuck was in the wrong. And I don't know that we were in the right going at him the way we did but sometimes things just happen that way. Like one second, you're standing still. And then . . . everything's moving fast-forward. Not real sure how you got there, but there it is."

Johnny Lee was smart, no doubt. He was in all the honors classes. Read insatiably like Christina. But I'd never heard him speak much. Especially not like that. Suddenly I realized why Ricky and him made sense. They were thinkers. Quiet and hidden.

"You know, Ricky really likes you," he said, squirting waves of mayo on his patty. "He's not messing with your head."

"Then why didn't he ever talk to me 'til now?"

Johnny Lee wrestled around in his seat before tearing open the packet of mustard with his teeth. "Intimidated. Not everybody's what you think they are, you know? On the outside." He crisscrossed lines of mustard on top of the mayo. "I mean, come on, Michelle. You really think my face looks like this from Chuck and those guys? I mean they got in a few swings but . . ." He chomped a couple potato chips. "You remember when I dragged into English class after regionals. Cast on my arm. And my face looked like it had a baseball bat taken to it, right?"

I nodded.

"I got laid out of the game on account of a head injury. It's funny how people don't put things together or just decide to look the other way. At least my old man didn't break my throwing arm." He clenched his right fist, open-shut. "That was all I kept thinking when he snapped the other one."

"Are you serious? That was your dad?"

Johnny Lee dropped his head—"Yeah"—and bit into another chip.

"But yesterday—I don't get it," I said. "He hit you because you got into a fight?"

"No. Ricky's a *Mexican* and I got into that fight with

Chuck because of a *Mexican*—and because . . ." He stopped himself, looking away from me.

" 'Cause of me. Michelle Owens, white trash."

"Hey, we're not high rollers on South Petra Street either. That's just a bunch of crap in my old man's head to make him feel like he's still king. Look, Michelle—I didn't mean to go off like this. Whining and all. I just—not everything is how it looks. Especially Ricky. He's a real swell guy."

"Swell?" I said with a kind of laugh.

"Yeah. Swell. And I think he thought, when your dad . . ." He paused. "I guess he thought he had something in common to talk about with you."

"Death?"

Johnny Lee shrugged.

"It's a little morbid," said Johnny Lee. "But his grandmother was his world. He gets it. Loss."

"Would you do it again?" I said.

"What?"

"Get in that fight with Chuck."

He considered the question with a chip hovering right at the edge of his lips.

"Yeah," he said. "I would. I believe fighting's wrong. But . . . you see, Ricky's my best friend. He's my family. That's what counts."

I rested my cheek against my fist, watching Johnny Lee stack chips inside his burger and in one motion gently smash the bun on top . . . no ashy print.

I knew something was up when I saw Uncle Jack's expression after school in the parking lot.

"What's wrong?" I asked, getting into his car.

"Put on your seat belt."

I snapped it on and we pulled away from the school.

"Well . . . ?" I said, with growing impatience.

"Danny came by the junior high."

I stiffened my back against the soft seat.

"He's decided to leave," said Uncle Jack. "Thinks it's what you want and what's best for you right now."

"When?"

"Day after tomorrow," said Uncle Jack. "Could be sooner. He said he had some things to do."

"Is he going back to Wisconsin?"

"Didn't say where," Uncle Jack said, stopping at a red light.

I was finally getting what I wanted, to be rid of Danny. I hadn't had to put up with him for a week, even though every single minute felt like an hour. So why wasn't I jumping for joy?

"I'm going to be straight with you, Mickey. And I'll make this the last of it. I still think you need to settle whatever this is between you two. I don't mean fix it. You can't fix six years in a couple of days. But sometimes—sometimes we just have to say what's really on our minds. In our hearts. You follow?"

I stared down at my sneakers. "Yeah, I guess," I said.

"You've lost a lot," he said. "Don't lose your brother too."

"You act like it's all my fault," I said.

"No, darlin'. I hope I act like it's no one's fault. Sometimes things just happen. Do you know that?"

I rested my head against the warm window as the car moved forward. The sky was a dull white-blue—not a single thing to wish on.

"I don't get it," I said.

"Get what?"

"How you can forgive Danny," I said, turning to Uncle Jack. "He treated you like dirt after the stadium. And Aunt Sara. She . . . when he quit coming around, I know it broke her good, Uncle Jack. Have you forgotten that?"

"No, Mickey. I haven't forgotten. But I know he was just—just a boy who had to be a man in a way he didn't expect to be."

"A man. Right, you think he grew up." I dropped my head back onto the window. "Ditching and running. That ain't growing up."

Uncle Jack stayed quiet. I tilted my head and watched him struggle to straighten his back against his seat. Really working to stretch his neck some. The same way he had the day of the storm.

"I lied to you," I said, knowing I had to come clean. "I lied when I smiled while you were fixing dinner the other night and you asked what I was thinking."

"What were you thinking?" he asked, turning a corner.

"Honest?" I said.

"Always honest," he said, with a gentle smile.

"I was thinking how tired you looked." I paused, unsure if I should say the rest. "She's never coming back, Uncle Jack. No matter how well you keep things in the same place."

He nodded.

"It's a hard thing. Letting go. If it were easy, we'd just do it. But it's not that simple. Loss just isn't simple, Mickey."

Uncle Jack was right about a lot of things. Almost everything. But he was wrong about one thing. I'd lost everything and I'd let go.

That afternoon I sat at the desk in my room at Uncle Jack's, staring at a page of trig. It seemed as foreign as Hebrew or Russian right then. My head was full of so much noise. What was I supposed to do? Beg Danny to stay? Tell him it was okay, that being nuts was fine? It wasn't.

Uncle Jack knocked on my door, startling me.

"Sorry to interrupt," he said. "You left this on the porch yesterday. Thought I'd bring it up."

He set *The Outsiders* on the edge of my nightstand.

"I'm heading into town," he said. "You need anything?"

I shook my head.

"All right. Don't study yourself cross-eyed."

"I won't."

I turned back to my homework, feeling less inspired than before. After a few minutes, I heard Uncle Jack's tires as he cut out of the driveway. I twisted back around in my chair and stared at *The Outsiders* lying like a wounded bird across the room from me.

I closed my textbook, walked over to the nightstand and hovered over that busted-up book. When I finally picked it up, it felt lighter than I ever remembered. Like if I opened it up, the pages might be empty. I plopped on the edge of my bed, flipping through it. As I went through, I remembered that cool energy of knowing about the Socs and the Greasers. Knowing about a place where brothers were heroes and sticking to your gang meant the world. Since

The Outsiders, I'd read so many books, but nothing, and I mean nothing, made me believe that I could make it out of that town and be something like that book.

I turned the page and saw that off to the right of Robert Frost's "Nothing Gold Can Stay" Danny had written STAY GOLD, MICHELLE. I shut the book and tossed it in my nightstand drawer. I sat back at my desk and opened my trig book.

No way. I wasn't Ponyboy. I wasn't gold.

17

When Uncle Jack got back, I borrowed his car to drop off *The Outsiders* for Danny. I didn't see any reason for me to keep it. I didn't need it any more than I needed Danny. They were one and the same as far as I was concerned.

I sat in the car and stared at the house for a while before I finally got out. The flag was up on the mailbox and inside was a small white envelope addressed to Iola, Wisconsin. I slid *The Outsiders* into my back pocket when a wave of the Beach Boys' "Surfin' Safari" echoed through the raised house windows. Dad . . .

I tossed the letter back in the mailbox and ran through the gate, swinging the screen door open. Music blaring.

There were half-packed cardboard boxes in the living room. Dad's bedroom door was open. I kicked through the box brigade littering the hallway. I stopped a foot from the door. My heart pounded in my ears. My stomach swelled in my throat. I stepped to the edge of the doorway and Danny was inside packing up Dad's room.

"What the hell are you doing?" I shouted over the music.

He lowered the volume on the record player.

"I'm packing. I figure it's a lot for you to do."

"How can you do this? I know you hate him, but how can you—"

"I do. I don't know how to be different about him, Michelle. But because you love him I don't think it's right to expect you to do this. I mean, can you honestly tell me you can pack all this stuff up without falling apart?"

"Have you *seen* me fall apart?" I asked, stepping into the room and slipping the needle off the record. "Don't ever confuse us. I ain't afraid to face the things that scare me."

I carefully tried to slip the record back in its cover. My hands shook. Why did they shake?

"You ever see this?" he asked. "I found it at the bottom of his nightstand drawer."

"Get out, Danny. Just leave everything."

"Look," he demanded, sliding the frame in front of me.

I'd never seen it. Not that I remembered. It was a picture of all of us together. Mom and Dad stood arm and arm beneath the hackberry tree out front. Dad was beaming. Really beaming. Mom had the warmest smile and the softest yellow sundress. I had on this stupid straw hat with a drooping

sunflower and Danny flexed his pretend bicep with a football cocked under his other arm. We looked like the kind of
family that could've come with the frame.

I held the record close to me. "Stay out of his stuff,"
I said.

He propped the picture on the nightstand. My throat
tightened. My eyes watered up. It was all I could do to look
at the records, the pictures, his work clothes, toolbox in the
corner—that was it. Forty-five years, and all he left was stuff.
Stuff I couldn't even bear to hold, to touch, to look at. What
happened? He'd gotten it together. We'd figured it all out.
He wasn't—why were my hands shaking—

"Michelle?"

Danny said my name the way I imagined Ponyboy's
brother Sodapop had said his after Johnny died. Suddenly I
was remembering *The Outsiders* like the Pledge of Allegiance
or the "Star-Spangled Banner." Ponyboy's voice felt like
my own:

>**I backed up just like a frightened
animal, shaking my head.
"I'm okay." I felt sick. I felt as if any
minute I was going to fall flat on my
face, but I shook my head. . . .**

"Mickey?" Danny stepped toward me.

I backed up to the doorway—rushed to my room. The
air was so tight. So thin. I clutched that record.

>**My heart was pounding in slow thumps,
throbbing at the side of my head, and
I wondered if everyone else could hear it.**

I locked the door and leaned against it to hold myself up. It was all coming too fast. I closed my eyes, trying to count to ten. At least to five. The numbers rammed into each other. I couldn't slam the brakes. I couldn't stop.

"Michelle, open the door," Danny said, shoving on it.

I could do trig, even physics, but I couldn't count to five? I couldn't get there between the sound of laughter— between . . .

"Mickey!" Danny beat on the door.

Then everything I was supposed to know for the quiz on T. S. Eliot. And the pamphlet "Grief Is Okay, You Are Okay," and somewhere the number three wedged in my brain, and I thought, God, please, help me find the next number. I wasn't gonna crack, 'cause I was seventeen. I was seventeen and tan and strong and everything Danny was at that age. Only I didn't screw up and quit on everything, and I had every reason to. I tried to shake it out of my head but it just kept coming and coming. . . .

Two bottle rockets shot off, popping, shimmering streams of gold, red-blue down from the black sky.

"Cut it out," Danny said to Roland. "You wanna get the sheriff out here?"

"It's a new year, man . . . ," Roland said, chugging a can of beer. "Woo-hoo!"

Four . . . I got to the number four. What was next?

"Mickey." Danny pounded on my bedroom door. "Mickey, open the door."

"What are you doing?" Danny asked Roland.

Roland pulled out a gas can and some wood from the trunk of his Z28.

170

"I'm gonna take these torches and dip 'em in gas, man. Cool, right? Then tie them to the stadium posts. The guys will eat it up. . . ."

"Try not to burn the place down, kamikaze," Danny said.

"Owens, chill." Roland reached in the passenger window of our pickup, belched in my face and pinched my nose. "What do I got? Your nose."

"You're so wasted," I said. I was sitting there reading The Outsiders.

"You're so wasted," he mocked.

All I could do was repeat: Four four four four—I didn't want to see. I couldn't see, please—why couldn't I get to—I couldn't breathe. There was too much—

"Hey, Mickey, check this out!" Roland shouted, laughing.

I turned—Roland was—the whole stadium lit up. Roland was— the can had leaked . . . he had spilled it—something . . . something.

No—get out get out get out get out—*Get out of my head!* I covered my ears with my hands but I could hear . . .

"Danny . . . !" Roland screamed.

He tumbled down the stands—burning. Danny ran.

"Mickey, get help! Hurry!"

I couldn't move. My hands were . . .

Shaking.

Five.

The number came into my head, and I opened my eyes.

"Mickey!" Danny pounded on the door. "I'll kick it in."

I unlocked the door and set the record down on the bed.

Danny came in as I opened the nightstand drawer and pulled out the picture of him graduation night.

"What are you . . . what the hell was that about?"

I stood there looking down at the picture of Danny. The deadness in his eyes, my eyes.

"What do you want me to do, Michelle? You want me to stay? To go? What? Answer me."

"I want you to make it better—to make it like it was before the fire. Only you can't. Do you even realize that, Danny? You can't," I said.

"You don't understand what it's been like," Danny said.

"I don't?" I asked.

"He was my *best* friend, Mickey."

I shoved him as hard as I could in the chest. "I was your sister, you jerk. You were *my* best friend!"

My glassy eyes watered up. I swallowed deep, trying to hold back the tears. And just when I thought I might hold it all in, a crash of warm wet plummeted down my hot face. He reached for me.

"Don't touch me, Danny," I said, turning away.

"Fine."

"Shut up with your fine."

"What do you want me to say?"

"I was there. I want you to say that I was there too. That . . ."

"What? What . . . ?" he said.

"It was me. Don't you get it?" I choked on tears. "I saw him first."

My skin was burning up and I wanted to rip right out of it, but all I could do was stand there covered in tears and sweat.

"Michelle, you couldn't have—"

"I heard him laughing . . . and if I wasn't looking at that *stupid* book . . . if I could've screamed one second sooner. . . . But I couldn't make a sound. I saw him burning and my mouth opened and I couldn't. And I thought, maybe you would've gotten there faster. Maybe . . . maybe he wouldn't have died."

"It wasn't your fault—you couldn't have done anything. Dontcha get it?"

"Oh, 'cause it's all your fault, right? Big-time martyr."

"There's nothing you could've—"

"There's nothing you could've done either, but look at you," I said. "You took the blame. You quit."

"I didn't quit," he snapped.

"You quit on me and Aunt Sara and Uncle Jack—you quit on Dad."

"He hated me!"

"So maybe he did hate you. So what?" I shook. "You quit everything. . . ."

"This town quit *me*, Mickey. I'd go down the streets and I knew what they were thinking."

"No you didn't."

"Yes I did!" He paused. "Murderer. It was my idea to be there that night. You hear me! My idea."

"You couldn't have made Roland quit being the irresponsible ass he always was—"

"Don't say that."

"He was."

Danny grabbed me by both arms, shaking me hard. "Don't say that about him."

"You kept him grounded. Just like Mr. Weldon said that day. But you didn't tell him to light the torches, Danny."

He saw his hands squeezing me too tight. He let go and dropped his head against the wall.

"I waited for you, Danny. I waited for you to come home."
I couldn't stop crying. " 'Til I couldn't. I had to take everything
about that night, about everything, and hold it in this quiet
little place inside of me or I would've just stopped breathing."
I inhaled and exhaled, shaking. "Why can't you see?"

"What? What do you want me to see?" he said, turning
to me. "I came back, Mickey. I'm right here."

I made for the door, and he stepped in front of me.

"Move," I demanded.

"I came back," he pleaded.

"No you didn't," I said. "You're so stupid."

"What?"

"You keep saying you're my brother. My brother died
that night. You're just the guy who gets to walk around in his
skin. 'Cause you look like him, but you ain't him."

I walked away from the door and sat on the windowsill.

"Uncle Jack says it's a hard thing, letting go. Only just
recently have I really seen how hard it is for him. So, I can
see"—I struggled—"it must've been hard for you. But I'm
still mad, Danny. I'm pissed off that you won't be my big
brother and face it. And you have no idea what this all has
done to me or Mr. Gonzalez or the people in town— Don't
turn away! You look at me. You raise your head for once." I
gave up on acting like I wasn't cut right up the middle, 'cause
I was. "Roland died. It's everyone's fault—it's no one's fault.
Just do me a favor and don't say I don't understand. I may
not know what it's like for you, but I sure know what the
last six years have been like for me. And maybe I thought
I was over it, but it haunts me. It haunts me that I couldn't—

174

get help fast enough. That I didn't make you talk to me afterward."

He crouched against the door frame with tears flooding his face. "There's nothing you could've done," he said, dropping his head into his hands.

I'd seen my brother cry twice. Once when he realized Mom would never come back, and right then. He didn't cry like some spoiled brat in the checkout line wanting one of a dozen pieces of candy. He didn't even cry the way people do on TV. He cried the way Uncle Jack did when Aunt Sara died. The kind of crying that comes from somewhere deep that seems endless.

"I kept thinking it over and over," Danny said. "You know, like in the book. Dally saves Johnny."

"Dally didn't save Johnny, Danny," I said, pulling *The Outsiders* from my back pocket. "He saved Pony."

He wiped his tears off with the neck of his T-shirt. I pitched the book across the room to him.

"That's why you can't read just the parts you like," I said.

Danny picked up the book and fanned the pages.

"You said there were no happy endings," he said.

"Yeah, well, there aren't." My lip quivered.

"Maybe it's 'cause it doesn't end," he said, tossing the book onto the floor.

There it was, *The Outsiders* sitting between us. A bridge I didn't know if I wanted to cross—could cross.

"What do you think?" he said.

I didn't say anything. He got up off the floor.

"You hungry?"

I shook my head.

"You want me to stop packing his room?"

I shook my head again.

He walked out, closing the door behind him. I kept staring at that book until I broke. Sobbed so hard that my insides felt like they'd cry right out. Right out and live in the pages of that book forever.

18

Uncle Jack was waiting for me when I came in the front door that night.

"Hey, girl," he said, and before he got the papers he was grading onto the end table, I started crying all over again.

What was wrong with me?

He got up off the sofa and wrapped his sturdy arms around me. A hurricane could blow everything down around us and he would've held me steady.

"He called," said Uncle Jack.

I kept crying. Couldn't stop.

"Oh, darlin' . . . shhh . . ." He placed his hand on the back of my head. "You're home now."

Home. Home? I pushed away from him.

"What?" he said.

I looked around the living room. The mantel covered in picture frames. The bowl of wise sayings. The perfectly polished floors. The entryway to the big kitchen.

"Mickey, talk to me."

I stepped into the dining room and placed my palm on the table. We hadn't had a meal there since—since—

"She's dead," I said.

"Yes, honey."

"No, she's *really* dead."

Uncle Jack got uncomfortable. Shifted around in his stance as he held his palm to the back of the sofa for support.

"I don't know what to understand anymore, Uncle Jack. Do you?"

"What do you mean?" His words struggled to line up into a question.

"Home?"

He nodded.

We stood there bracing ourselves for some time. Then I felt it. I couldn't stretch into some stupid smile to make him feel better. I wasn't Mrs. Alvarado—I wasn't grown up in that way. Uncle Jack had been right. Only he didn't know it.

"She's dead," I said again, the words so choked they were almost whispers.

"Yes," he said, clearing his throat several times.

He moved around the arm of the sofa and sat down. I walked over and sat across from him on the love seat. We both looked at the bowl sitting in the center of the coffee table. Unsteady, his hand picked a slip of paper from the bowl. He studied its smallness in his palm before he carefully opened it.

"What's it say?"

Tears quietly shot down his cheeks. His breath was heavy and strained as he read, " 'Life is meant to be lived. Not waited on.' "

He wiped his nose and tried to smile at me. I didn't smile back. He cried harder.

I walked around the coffee table and sat beside him. I put my hand in his. And as scary as it was, I sat there with him as he bawled.

When I hit my pillow at Uncle Jack's that night, I thought I'd never wake up again. But it was around five-thirty the next morning when the phone went to ringing. My first thought: Danny. Danny drunk. Danny fighting. Then there was a gap in the half-asleep, half-awake . . . Danny dead.

A few minutes later, Uncle Jack knocked on my door.

"Come in," I said as the light of the hall spilled in behind him.

"Danny called. He wants to see you."

"When?" I said, turning on the lamp on the nightstand, squinting at the brightness.

"Said he'd be over in half an hour. I told him I'd talk to you first and call him back."

"Why's he coming?"

"He's catching the seven-fifteen bus."

I stared at the foot of my bed.

"You don't have to see him," said Uncle Jack.

"I know." I shrugged. "But I will."

He nodded and before he could shut the door I said, "Uncle Jack. About last night. I didn't mean to . . . to hurt you."

"Always honest, right?" he said.

"Right."

"Sometimes honesty hurts. And it doesn't mean it's a bad thing, Mickey."

I nodded.

"I'm gonna call your brother," he said, shutting the door behind him.

What was meant to be thirty minutes was more like ten as I heard Danny pull up in the pickup. From my bedroom window, I watched him emerge with damp hair and that blue jean jacket, flicking his cigarette in front of him and stamping it out with the toe of his boot. He looked like someone cool and famous, how he took a deep breath and closed his eyes, dropping his head just a little back—Christina would've said he was praying. Maybe he was. But it made me think of all the photographers who useta shout, "Hold it! That's it, that's real," when Danny was bound for football greatness.

Only thing was, this time there were no camera guys—reporters. No crowds, no cheers . . . no one to pose for. Danny stood there holding that look without any inkling that I was watching—waiting for him to step out of the newspaper clipping and onto the porch. I wanted it to all be over and figured he wanted the same.

He eventually stepped toward the house and disappeared just short of the porch. I didn't move.

There were footsteps up the stairs. A knock on my door. A sloppy boy's knock. I turned from the window, suddenly thinking I could duck out of it. But how? He was here. There. Outside my door.

He knocked again.

I walked over and put my hand on the doorknob. Twisted it right. Pulled . . .

And there he stood.

"Hey," he said.

"Hey."

"You think I can come in? Or you could come out."

I stepped back, opening the door wide. He walked in, eyeing the details.

"This is real nice," he said.

"Yeah, it's good."

We stood there awkwardly for a moment.

"So you're leaving."

"Yup."

"Well, I guess . . . I'll see ya," I said.

He nodded.

"This is a good desk here," he said, walking across the room. He tapped the top with his knuckles. "Bet you get a lot of work done here. Computer and calculator and everything."

"I do okay."

"This room is so big. Not like at our place, huh?"

I dropped my head. "It's not really about the size."

"No, no—of course. No." He stepped toward me. "But the room. It's nice, huh?"

I looked at him. "Yeah, it's nice, Danny," I said with my hand still on the door.

He nodded. He was nervous. Plenty nervous.

"Well, I better get going."

He started out and stopped in the doorway.

"I was thinking maybe you'd want to go with me."

"On the bus?"

"No—to the station. Maybe we could talk. Or just sit."

"I got school."

"Yeah, but not 'til eight, right? I'll be gone by then. And you could take the truck."

I felt anxious. Uneasy. There was nothing more to say. And sit? Sit and what, wait?

"You don't have to. . . ." He rolled the toe of his boot on the floor. "I just thought we could."

"I'll go."

"Huh?"

"Just wait outside the door." He didn't follow. "So I can get dressed."

"Okay." And there he went. Right outside the door.

I kicked into a pair of jeans and threw on a T-shirt. Socks and then my sneakers. I stopped midway while tying my shoes. Was I really doing this? Why was I doing this? My mouth was opening to say, "I changed my mind," when I reeled the phrase back in with a breath.

"You can come in," I said, continuing to tie my shoe. "Just a couple more seconds."

He nodded, standing in the doorway as I stuck my books into my backpack and flung it over my shoulder.

"Don't you need your calculator?" he said.

"Huh? Oh no. I do most of it in my head."

I turned off the lamp and waited for him to move out of the doorway. He was sitting on something to say. For the life of me, I couldn't have told you if I really wanted to know or not.

"We should probably go," I said.

"Right. Go."

He walked out, and I looked around the room. Then shut the door.

We came downstairs and Uncle Jack was drinking coffee at the dining room table with the paper sprawled out. It was the first morning as far as I could remember that he wasn't sitting at the kitchen table drinking out of Aunt Sara's yellow mug.

"You two ready for some breakfast?" he asked, as if we were both heading off to school.

"Danny asked me to go to the Kwik 'N' Go with him," I said, as Uncle Jack made his way toward us.

"If that's fine by you, Uncle Jack," said Danny.

Uncle Jack nodded and grinned and it was solid real. "Sure, son. It's fine."

"I'll pick her up some breakfast on the way there," Danny said.

We headed out but Danny stopped with the screen door propped open. He turned and held out his hand to Uncle Jack.

"Thanks," Danny said.

I stood between them as they shook hands. I didn't get what Danny was saying thanks for exactly, but I don't think it mattered 'cause Uncle Jack did.

I thought Danny would've had more to say on the ride into town, but he didn't. He pulled into the drive-thru at

Pronto Tacos and ordered us two potato-and-egg breakfast tacos apiece. An extra chorizo-and-egg for him. When we pulled up to the Kwik 'N' Go, I hopped out with the paper bag of tacos and sat on a bench facing the gas pumps. It wasn't too long before he followed, dropping his duffel beside me.

"Be right back," he said. "Gotta go get my ticket."

I reached in the white bag, pulling out the tiny plastic salsa containers and brown napkins, and opened my steaming potato-and-egg taco. I salivated. I'd just finished dousing it with pepper and salsa and had my first big bite when Danny came out of the gas station's glass doors. He plopped on the bench and held out a plastic bottle of Vanilla Coke.

"Thanks," I said.

"It ain't as good as the ones from the DQ," said Danny. "But thought you'd like it anyway."

He took off his jacket and flung it over his duffel.

"It's gonna be a hot one," he said, unscrewing the Coke cap.

He was right. It wasn't even six-thirty and it felt like it was eighty degrees.

"Guess you're all set," I said.

"Yup. Left the keys in the glove box."

"Thanks."

I heaved out a deep breath, and we sat there both feeling pretty awkward.

"You gonna eat?" I asked.

"Yeah . . ." He reached in the bag, then stopped. "I'll wait 'til I get on the bus. Long ride."

"You gonna tell me where you're heading?" I said, swallowing a mouthful of food.

"Wisconsin."

I finished off the taco, wadded up the foil and reached in for my second one.

"How come you never ask me why Wisconsin?" said Danny.

"I don't know," I said, pouring a thick layer of salsa on the taco. "You tucked that letter away pretty fast. Didn't seem to really want to talk about it."

He reached in the bag again, this time pulling out a potato-and-egg. He tore off edges of the tortilla, chewing real slow. No question about it, he was ready to hatch something.

"Ask me," Danny said.

"What?"

"Why Wisconsin? Why not Tennessee or California or Arizona or the crazy house in Amarillo, 'cause that was actually true for about two months?"

He caught me off guard on the last part.

"You'd think you'd never run into anyone from Three Rivers some seven-hundred-odd miles away in Amarillo but that's the whole small-world thing, I guess."

I sat there staring at my taco. I'd wanted to know why Wisconsin since I saw that bus stub the day he arrived. And now, he dangled some bit of truth about where he'd come from and I wasn't biting.

"Ask me why Wisconsin," Danny said.

I looked at the truck not fifteen feet from me. Keys were in the glove box. I could go. I could. I didn't owe him anything. Not one damn thing. But there I was sitting right next to him. A bag of breakfast tacos and condiments was the only thing separating the two of us. That was it. I really could go. I felt myself edge toward the truck, then settle.

I wasn't gonna run.

When I looked back at him, he lifted his head, and those eyes, they weren't dead. They weren't the eyes in the picture I'd kept in my nightstand for the last six years.

"Okay. Why Wisconsin?" I said.

"I got a son," he said.

"What?"

He nodded. "I'd been out in Arizona for a while. Not really doing anything." He scratched the back of his head. "And I met this . . . woman. Her name's Kali. She was just supposed to be passing through. Vacationer, you know, Grand Canyon. But she . . . she helped me, Michelle. Not maybe in the same way coming back here has, but she reached . . . she didn't think my life was over." He took a swig of his Coke. "Anyway, she's from Wisconsin, so I moved there." He laughed. "It's pretty damn cold."

I let loose a small smile. "I bet."

"See here," he said, reaching for his wallet. "That's her."

"She's pretty."

"Yeah."

"You married?" I said.

"No. But like I said, we have a son." He flipped through his wallet. "That's him when he was a couple months old. But he'll be two in July. On the Fourth."

"You name him Firecracker?" I joked.

Danny grinned. "No. We named him Mickey."

We didn't say much else during the forty-some-odd minutes we waited. When the bus pulled in, he hugged me something smothering. The air pushed all the way out of me, and his heart pounded so hard I could feel it against my chest.

When he finally let go, Danny squeezed my clammy hands real snug as a dozen thoughts bumper-car-crashed in my head. He was about to say something when—

"And how are we today, sir?" the bus driver asked Danny.

"Fine . . ." Danny cleared his throat, handing him his ticket.

The man ripped off a portion and gave Danny the remainder. "There you are, sir. And I'll remind you about your changeover in Dallas."

Danny nodded, slipping the ticket back in his jacket pocket, not realizing why the man was still waiting.

"Your bag," I said.

Danny slung it off his shoulder and handed it to him.

"So . . ." Danny said, head down, kicking his boot heel on the cracked pavement.

I held out the bag of tacos to him.

"Oh, yeah, thanks." Jittery, he took it and lightly slapped it against his leg.

He glanced over his shoulder as the bus driver slammed the luggage door shut and stepped back on the bus. That was Danny's cue. His cue to get on and leave.

"Well, I guess—" I said.

"Yeah," he interrupted, faking enthusiasm.

I stood there not knowing what to do. We'd hugged. We'd talked. And there it was still living. That gap—that space that hung thick and damp, and I sure didn't know how to fill it. From the looks of him he didn't either.

Then he let out this shaky breath and said, "I'll see ya real soon."

I crossed my arms around my waist as a school bus rolled past the gas station.

"I don't know how to forgive you yet, Danny. You know?"

He kept kicking his boot heel into the pavement. I didn't know if what I said would send him into a snap or numb him. But it was like Uncle Jack said to me, always honest. And that was honest.

He slid the bottom of his boot back and when it seemed he'd go without looking at me again, he raised his head. It was a hard thing for him, I could tell. To look at me like that. Without any kind of hiding. But he did it.

"Good luck with graduation. I'll be thinking about you, Michelle."

He climbed up the bus steps and it wasn't like in the movies or on TV. I could barely make out his face in the tinted dust-covered window where he took a seat. If I could've reached up high enough, I would've written WASH ME right where I imagined his chest was. I waited 'til the brake release let out like someone exhausted from holding their breath too long. Waited 'til the wheels slowly slid forward. Waited in case the storybook ending found its way to both of us and somehow everything in the last six years was resolved and we were like we'd been before the stadium burnt down. But the bus kept going and took a wide turn, exiting onto the road leading to the highway.

I hopped in the truck and looked over at the passenger seat. Danny had gone back to the Pizza Hut claw machine and got that brown plush bear. It sat there buckled in snug by the lap belt. I leaned over and popped the glove box open for the keys, and there they were . . . sitting on top of *The Outsiders*. I shot back up, gripping the steering wheel. My eyes fixed on that book. That broken spine. That tattered-edged cover. What was I so scared of?

Then I thought about last night and about that slip of paper out of Aunt Sara's bowl, and as cheesy as it was I even thought about that laminated poster on Mrs. Alvarado's office door.

LET THE EXCELLENCE IN YOU SHINE THROUGH.

How lame was that? But I rounded back again to Aunt Sara. And Dad. And that photograph Danny'd held in front of me in Dad's room of all of us. We had been a family once. It wasn't just something in a dream. Did it fix everything to think of it that way? No way. No way around the moon and back. But it happened. Just as much as what did at the stadium.

I snapped up the book and the keys. Turned over the ignition. *Humm* . . .

When I ran my hand over the cover of *The Outsiders,* I felt something. Something I couldn't put words to right then.

19

At lunch, Christina was nowhere to be found, so I grabbed a sandwich, a bag of chips, and a can of Pepsi and crouched on a ledge behind the gym. While I ate, fire ants bubbled up from a hole in the ground, scattering in these zigzags. Just as the thought of how miserable the last few weeks of school would be without Christina really settled in, a voice said, "Hey."

Ricky stood with his hands jammed in his baggy jeans' back pockets. His sexy jet-black hair draped one side of his face.

With my cheek full of sandwich and chips, a garbled "Hey" squeezed out between my lips.

"I saw you take off from the caf. Wasn't sure . . . to follow but . . . can I?" He motioned to the ledge beside me.

I nodded, washing down my food with a gulp of Pepsi.

"So . . . you gonna yell at me again?" he asked. "Just wanted to be ready for it this time."

"No." I dusted an ant off my sneaker.

"Cool. . . . Why did you yell at me, again?"

"Things just haven't made a lot of sense." I picked at the bread crust.

"Sure. Yeah. I mean, sure," he said. "Like I said, it was stupid to ask if I could kiss you given what you're going through. I just sort of—thought it and—said it."

"So you didn't mean it?" I asked.

"No. I mean, yeah, I did." He dropped his head, running his hands through his hair. "But I really meant to be your friend that day—every day. Even though you said some really uncool stuff about my grandmother."

He shuffled a toe of his Vans across the scratchy dirt sidewalk.

"Yeah, I'm sorry about that too. I was kind of on the edge of a nervous—something."

We both looked down at our shoes.

"I mean, it's not an easy . . . what you gotta go through. It makes sense, you know? That things feel a little . . . loose. So I forgive you. 'Cause of that and 'cause . . . I think you're really cool."

He blushed. Ricky "The Ghost" Martinez blushed in front of me—because of me. Had the earth stopped moving?

"So," he said.

"So."

"So . . . this will probably sound kind of weird but . . . you know the school dance?"

"I don't actually go to those."

"Yeah, me neither really. I went freshman year with a senior and all the guys hassled me. So Johnny Lee and me usually go stag or just hang out at the Dairy Queen." He paused, twisting the toes of his Vans in. "But I was thinking . . ." He blew air out the side of his mouth. "Maybe you and Christina could hang with us. I mean, if you wanted."

There my face went grinning like crazy. Of course we'd go. Then I remembered.

"Kind of all hinges on whether or not Christina ever talks to me again. And I'm not really sure how to fix it. How lame is that?"

"Maybe play it cool."

"What do you mean?" I said.

He slipped a Ruffle out of my chip bag. "I mean, it's kind of your fault, right?"

"Yeah?"

"Then . . . just say you're sorry."

"I said that."

"Yeah, but, it's like when I piss off Johnny Lee . . . I have to make up for it. In a way that's real. Because we're best friends—like forever."

"Yeah," I said. "Like forever."

He smiled and chomped another chip. "Besides. She's been hiding out on the other side of the gym at lunch."

"Shut up."

"I'm serious. You two keep this up and everyone will be sitting out here. It's ninety-two degrees. That's way too hot."

The bell rang.

"Wow, that was fast," he said.

The bell rang again. And again.

"Fire drill," I said.

Ricky and I headed for the parking lot as everybody poured out of the cafeteria.

"Something must really be burning," he said.

"What do you mean?"

"Since when do we have a fire drill at lunch?"

Everyone clustered up into their cliques as we all looked around for smoke . . . for fire. Johnny Lee picked through the crowd and made his way over to us.

"Hey, man, what's up?" Ricky said to him.

"What's going on?" Johnny Lee said. "Hey, Michelle."

"Don't know, man. You see anything?"

Johnny Lee shook his head. "Just a lot of teachers running around."

I stepped up on the tips of my toes and peered over the crowd. It wasn't long before I saw Christina standing by herself. As by herself as she could get with a schoolful of students and teachers all around. Her nose characteristically buried in a book with a look that said she'd rather be at one of her mother's church meetings than standing there.

"Hey," I said to Ricky. "I'll catch up with you."

"Cool."

I peeled through the crowd. Bumping a few people by accident on my way to Christina. Then some guy shoved me as he caught a football and I fell into someone.

"Sorry," I said to the guy, and soon as he pulled me back to my feet, I froze.

Right beside him was . . . That Kid. That Kid who had killed Dad.

The air went right out of me.

"Hi," he squeaked out.

"Hey."

He really was a kid. All soft around the edges with tender eyes and neatly combed dark hair. His arm cast was decorated with X-Men stickers and drawings of bug-eyed caricatures. Hardly any signatures, though. Only one that I could see.

"Um," he said, as if suddenly forgetting a speech he'd rehearsed. "I know I'm not supposed to talk to you in case you want to sue my parents but . . ." His eyes shot all over the place. "I'm . . . what happened—I swear I didn't mean it. I didn't see him coming and"—That Kid's eyes couldn't steady—"I never cut school and well, I didn't mean it."

Some part of me wanted to rip him in two, and I could've. He was scared of me and that suddenly seemed like a lot to have over a person. A whole lot.

I looked at the girl beside him. The same girl I'd seen with him in the hallway. She was probably Ricky's cousin. Her eyes were just as kind as Ricky's. And she was definitely crushing on That Kid.

"How's your arm?" I asked him.

He looked at it as if he'd forgotten it was broken. "It itches mostly."

"My brother broke his leg once," I said. "Straighten a wire hanger and try that."

Just as he was about to say something, the principal spoke over a bullhorn.

"Sorry, everyone. False alarm. False alarm. Everyone head back to lunch for an extra fifteen minutes."

There was a moment of cheering and clapping before

194

everyone streamed back toward the school. That Kid's friend nudged him and he followed her lead. Before they got too far, he stopped and turned back.

"Th-thanks," he stammered.

"Sure."

He dipped his head and dropped into the herd of students. Watching him disappear, I thought about everything else I could've said. That Kid was the reason Dad swerved. Still, it just didn't make sense somehow to shred him, and I didn't know why.

When I finally turned to find Christina, she'd already gone.

"Everything cool?" Ricky said from behind me.

I turned, nodding at him and Johnny Lee. "I hope so."

I looked for Christina between classes but she'd pretty much perfected a stealthy avoidance method. Stealthy enough to avoid me anyway. After my last class, I rushed to her locker, but she never showed. So I took off down the hallway toward mine. Halfway there, I caught Chuck's eyes tracking me over the shoulders of the Lettermans huddled around him. Weaving through the crowded hall, I kept my eyes low until I reached my locker.

I popped the handle, cramming my seventh-period books and a spiral into the mess inside. Grabbed my history folder and trig book and stuck them in my backpack. Just as I was about to close my locker, *The Outsiders* caught my eye from the top shelf, its taped-together binding facing out. Locker doors slammed shut. Students trickled out the door at the end of the hall, laughing . . . gossiping. It all fell off as

I shouldered my backpack and reached for the book. Fanning the pages, I stopped where Danny had written:

Stay Gold, Michelle

Where was he? Traveling through Waco? Amarillo? Crunched up on a bus beside a woman who talked endlessly about her cat while he tried to read *Sports Illustrated* or some newspaper he picked up off the seat when he got on? Was he thinking about flinging burgers in Arizona? Was he thinking about me? *Stay gold.* He couldn't stay gold and he was as gold as they came.

I dropped the book into my backpack and zipped it. Soon as I spun away from my locker, I collided right into Chuck. It wasn't one of those accidental bump-intos. He'd been hovering . . . waiting. I buried my head and said sorry while stepping around him.

He snatched hold of my upper arm.

"Let go, Chuck," I said, half frustrated, half afraid.

Kids walked around us, a few craning their necks.

"I want to ask you something."

My jaw clenched.

"See, I think you might be confused. Because of what happened in the cafeteria."

Now the students that hadn't left were getting an eyeful as they propped against their lockers. My cheeks were burning hot.

"What?" I asked.

"You think Ricky wants something *real* from you?"

A jolt of adrenaline ripped through my veins.

"Hey, Chuck, we're gonna be late," shouted one of the Lettermans from the end of the hall.

"In a second," Chuck shouted back.

"Is this the part where I say real like *what?*" I held my jaw firm but didn't meet his eyes. "Or just try to read your mind?"

He leaned in, his grip tightening. I winced.

"Don't kid yourself, Mickey. Only *real* thing he wants from white trash like you is bragging rights for banging a freak-virgin."

Chuck wanted to get a rise out of me—needed to. And guess what? He did. Because something inside me clicked, and I couldn't believe I looked that prick straight in the eye and said, "It really does bother you that everyone thinks you're gay, doesn't it?"

And that *slapped* the smirk right off his chiseled face.

"Or maybe it's just that you can't stand that everyone likes Ricky because he *is* real and you"—I chuckled—"you're the most scared person in this entire town."

I held his gaze.

"Oh, I think your brother holds the lead in the town chicken-shit category." He smirked again, sure that he had me good.

"Well, then you're running a close second."

"What did you say?"

I gulped. "You can't make me cry anymore, Chuck." I leaned into him. "And if you don't let go of my arm, I swear I'll kick you so hard in the balls you won't wear Wranglers for a month."

I didn't so much as blink, but my legs trembled. Until that redneck had whispered in my face at the cafeteria, I hadn't been that close to Chuck L. Nelson since we kissed in sixth grade.

Chuck looked up to see if anyone had followed along.

Guess everybody had lost interest way before my speech because only the Lettermans at the end of the hall were watching. They looked impatient more than anything. One of the guys pointed to his watch.

Chuck's squeeze let loose. Blood rushed to where his hand had been clamped.

As he walked down the hall and disappeared out the door, I didn't have one of those cheesy moments where everyone starts clapping for standing up to the school bully. They went on doing whatever they had been doing before. The moment happened and then it was over.

When I came out the double doors leading to the parking lot, I actually saw Christina waiting for the school bus. An ultimate self-deprecating low, as she loathed riding the bus. My adrenaline was still pumping from Chuck's crap. So after a few deep breaths, I jogged down the steps and stood beside her. I dangled the truck keys in front of her face. She walked away from me.

"Come on, Christina."

She pulled out a book and sat on a pipe railing.

"Go away, Gringa."

I scooched in beside her. She slid away.

I scooched. She slid. I started to scooch again—

"Cut it out," she snapped.

I eased back down on the railing and stayed quiet for a moment. Buses began turning into the parking lot.

"You can't ride the bus. You'll never forgive yourself," I said.

"Now you get to tell me what to do?" she said, not raising her head from her book. "You gonna tell me how to feel next?"

"Look, I'm sorry," I said.

"Heard that one."

I felt myself choking up, getting teary.

"I'm sorry, Christina. I don't know how to ask for help. That sounds so After School Special lame."

She looked at me long and hard over her book.

"Those better not be crocodile tears, Gringa."

I laughed. "No, Mexican, they're the real ones. The ones that say I don't want us to be like this."

"You really are hurtful, Mickey."

"I know."

"And sometimes a complete *pendeja*."

I nodded.

"And you can't think that's all it takes to make me forgive you? A ride?"

"What do you want me to say?"

"Say you actually care how much it hurt me when you snapped like some damn turtle when I tried talking to you. Say that you understand that I'm your best friend, and that it matters to you. Or at least say whatever stupid *gringas* say in all those After School Specials you hate so much."

"They say I'm sorry. Sorry that I didn't let you in. That I wanted to push everyone away because if they knew that I couldn't feel anything about my dad—about Roland—that they'd hate me. That you'd hate me."

She waited. The bus doors opened and students started pouring in. She stuffed the book in her purse and I figured it was over. And just when I almost got up to go, she said, "That's what they would say on those shows? No wonder you hate them. That's loco talk." She slid down toward me. "See, because best friends, they already know these things. They already know you're hurting. *¿Bueno?*"

"*Bueno,*" I said.

She stood up and held out her hand. "*Andale.* And I want you to know I'm only forgiving you 'cause I don't want to have to pray about it anymore."

"That's the only reason?" I said.

"*Ay,* don't push it," she said as we walked across the parking lot. "Or I'll make you repeat that whole After School Special thing again. What? Why are you laughing?"

"It's just good to have you annoy me again."

"Hey, question, Gringa: How did you talk your brother into loaning you the truck?"

"He's gone," I said, walking around the front of it.

She paused and looked at me before we both climbed in. I slid the key into the ignition but didn't turn over the engine.

"You okay?" she asked.

I shrugged.

"Wanna tell me later?" she said.

I nodded.

"Okay. But you *better* tell me every detail or I swear you'll eat alone the rest of the school year."

"I will. I *will.* . . ." I turned over the ignition, suddenly remembering lunch with Ricky.

"What?" she said. "I can see there's something else."

I dropped the gear into drive.

"What do you think about going to the school dance?"

"Serious?"

I looked up and nodded while I pulled out of the parking lot.

"I don't know. It's never been our scene."

"Maybe. Or maybe not."

"Gringa . . ."

"Maybe we'll do what we always do but with some company."

Her brow furrowed. I grinned.

"Spill it," she said.

"What do you think about maybe hanging with Ricky and Johnny Lee?" I said.

"No f-ing way! A double with the hottest guys in school? *Adio mio.*" She did the cross-kiss-crucifix thing. "Angie would spit fire. The whole school would spit fire."

"Well, Johnny Lee *is* a *gringo,*" I said, jokingly.

But her excitement suddenly fell off, and it wasn't because he was white. She'd never gone out with a guy. After that thing where that jerk tried to . . . after that, she'd talk about guys the way you do to seem normal. But the idea of really going on a date, no way.

"It's not a big deal," I said. "It was just an idea."

Then she grinned. "Shut up, Gringa. Not a big deal. I'll . . . go."

"Yeah?"

"*Ay,* I just won't tell my mom."

I didn't follow.

"That he's a *gringo.* Because if she lights one more candle for me this week, the church will probably burst into flames."

I started laughing.

"What?" she said.

"Nothing," I smiled, cranking up the radio. "Nothing at all."

20

"I should've brought a book," Christina said, smacking on her bubble gum. "This pretty-people-watching thing is boring this year. Someone should've already come out crying by now."

She and I sat at a picnic table outside the school dance, acting like we were watching TV while everyone was inside the cafeteria under icicle lights and glitter-dipped streamers—dancing or sitting at tables drinking punch and eating off miniplates. I'd gone to all the dances exactly like this. Sitting outside sipping a bottle of Coke with a wedge of lime, making wisecracks with Christina. Watching the drama unfold as a couple always broke up before the end of the night and came tearing out the glass doors. But this was my last high school dance, and I realized I didn't really know any of them. How did I go through three years and not know the other five hundred kids around me? Kids I'd grown up with. Not to mention I started thinking Ricky and Johnny Lee bumped into a reality check on their way to the dance and were tucked away in the cafeteria with a set of girly-girls.

"Christina, you ever think we should've gone into one of these things?" I said.

"Nope. It's much better as a spectator sport. Less chance of injury." She blew a bubble with her gum and popped it. "Hey, Mickey."

"Yeah."

"Promise me something."

I shrugged, nodding.

"Swear on The Virgin that you'll come back."

"What?" I laughed.

"Swear," she said, turning her leg toward me. "Swear on The Virgin that you'll come back to visit . . . at least for holidays and birthdays."

"Are you really freaking out?"

"*Ay,*" she said, facing herself forward on the bench again. "It's just gonna be all hard next year without you, Gringa."

Christina's finger outlined the knifed etching of Gina Rodriguez's name with a heart around it on the table. I'd never sworn on a virgin before but if it made Christina feel better . . .

"I swear," I said. "But I'm not gonna have to come back too much, 'cause you ain't gonna get stuck here. Christina . . ." I dropped into her eye-line. "You can get outta this town too."

"*Ay,* don't get all guidance counselor on me."

"Okay," I said, rocking her back and forth with my shoulder. "But I'm still gonna bug you about it."

She pushed back into me and there we went with our shoving war. What a couple of weirdos we were.

"Gringa, I'm gonna knock you off this bench. . . ."

"Hey," a voice called out.

Christina and I looked up and saw Ricky and Johnny Lee dead ahead. Ricky carrying a brown paper bag.

She leaned into me. "They really showed?"

And Ricky was . . . wow. His baggy khakis and button-down black shirt finished with polished black Doc Martens. Was he for real this good-looking and staring at me? Me in my University of Dallas T-shirt and blue jeans.

They sat across from us.

"Sorry we're late," Johnny Lee said, kind of shy, and lit up looking at Christina before I fell into his radar. "It was this guy over here."

"You look really nice," I said to Ricky. "Did you want to go in?" I reluctantly asked.

"No," he said. "I just . . ." He shrugged nervously. "It's what I had . . . to wear, you know."

"Don't let him fool you, Mickey. The guy spent over two hours trying on everything in his closet."

"Shut up, man," Ricky said, embarrassed.

Johnny Lee grinned, his attention falling back to Christina. "I just had T-shirts and jeans," he said to her with a little shame in his voice. "I hope that's all right."

She kept her eyes steady on him. Looking for some kind of trap . . . some hidden meanness. But he just sat there with his head tucked in a little, his fingers tracing the grooves on the table.

"Yeah," she said, smiling at him. "It's all right."

Christina smile like that at a guy? Now *that* is what her mother would call a divine miracle.

"Swell," he said, with that shy grin of his.

They started small-talking about something to do with a class as I awkwardly exchanged glances with Ricky. The notion of the two of us there on a "sort of date" suddenly intimidated me. I'd never been on a date. He'd been on—well, I didn't know how many, but I'd seen him with enough girls to know he knew more about dates than I did.

"Anyway," Christina said to the guys, "you'll wish you brought a book after about ten minutes of this people-watching. It's a slow night."

"I uh—I did," Johnny Lee said.

"Yeah?" Excited, Christina leaned across the table as he reached into his back pocket.

"It's this new book of Cuban poetry." Johnny Lee handed it to her. "Well, new but half-price."

She thumbed through the pages, straining to read it in the dim light.

"If you want, we could go sit on the gym steps," Johnny Lee said. "There's better light over there."

Christina hesitated for a moment, then looked at me. "Is that cool with you, Gringa?"

I wasn't sure I wanted her to go, but her giving a guy a chance not to be a jerk seemed important.

"Yeah," I said, smirking.

She leaned in and whispered, "You can settle those gossip gums because it's not like a hookup." She swung her leg off the bench.

And there the two of them went. And there I was. Alone with Ricky Martinez, who, for the first time, seemed more nervous than me as he shifted around on the bench.

"So . . . um, sorry about . . . being late."

"It's okay. We sit here every year anyway. Kind of a tradition, you know."

"Yeah. Oh, I almost forgot." He reached in the paper bag and pulled out a wrist corsage. "My mom picked it up 'cause I was kind of all over the place. You're not allergic, are you?"

"No," I said, surprised. "You told your mom you were meeting me here?"

"Yeah. Why?"

"Well, I don't exactly fall into the category of the spaghetti-strap, high-heel-wearing girls inside," I said, nodding toward the cafeteria.

He turned around and saw a cluster of cheerleaders standing by the windows with their dates. The twinkling lights made it easier than usual for them to be small-town princesses.

He shy-smiled, turning back around. "You still think I care about that?"

I dropped my head.

"No. Maybe—it's just . . ."

He waited.

"You look nice," I said.

"You could say handsome." He reached across the table and slid the corsage on my wrist. "But nice is cool."

I held up my arm and inspected the difference something that soft and delicate could make.

"So . . . what do you think?" he asked.

"About?"

He bit his lower lip. "Me getting to dance with you."

I blushed. Thank god it was pretty dark.

"I don't wanna go in there," I said.

"Me neither."

"Dance out here?" I said.

He grinned and said, "Yeah," sliding off the bench. "We got all these stars. It's a lot better than those lights."

My stomach swam all over the place as he held his hand out for me to take. He was serious. How could he be serious about holding out his hand for me? But there it was. Waiting.

"Come on," he said.

Soon as I took his hand, I realized mine was beyond clammy—it was soaked. I wiped it off on my jeans while he brushed his fingertips over his lips, not saying a word.

"Sorry," I said.

He held out his hand again. I took it and as I got up he whispered, "It's cool . . . really."

As we walked away from the picnic tables, I fell right into step with him. The muffled music echoing from the cafeteria was a fast song but he held me in close. I'd *never* danced slow and close with a guy in my whole life but it came as natural as trig. At least with Ricky.

"What are you thinking?" he said.

"It's lame."

"Come on," he said, baiting me. "You know you wanna tell me."

"Okay . . . but no laughing."

"No way," he said.

"I was thinking about . . . Ah, it's stupid."

"So be stupid," he said. "You're safe. I'm filled with stupid."

"Right . . . okay. So . . ."

"So . . ."

"So one of the best times I ever had in school was when you flunked and ended up in my kindergarten class."

"And . . . is there an and?"

I kind of laughed. "Yeah, I . . ." A group of giggling girls came out of the dance. "My favorite part was when you'd sometimes get up on the little round yellow table in the corner. You remember the one by the window?"

"Oh yeah," he said, the thought washing over his face. "It had those . . . red and blue handprints on top."

"Yeah. And you'd stand up there reading your poems— telling stories. Mrs. Garcia trying to get you to sit down but you . . . were so . . . different." I paused. "Okay. That was way stupid. Erase that."

Sweat beads bubbled onto my upper lip.

"Why?" he asked, as I put my head back on his shoulder.

I shrugged. "I don't know."

A slow song came on and some people began fanning out of the cafeteria. When I started to pull away, he held on to me.

"Hey . . . ," he said.

"What?"

"Where you going?"

I dropped my head, jamming my hands into my back pockets.

"Don't you ever worry what people will think?" I said.

"What do you mean?"

"You know, Ricky 'The Ghost' Martinez hanging with Michelle Owens. I'm not exactly in your circle."

He half laughed. "Yeah, not really into the whole . . . circle thing. I mean, we've been dancing in a circle but . . . That was supposed to be funny. Okay. Seriously. You know what they'll think, Mickey? They'll think I'm hanging with the smartest, coolest, prettiest girl in school."

"No they won't," I said, looking toward the cafeteria. "Not in this town."

"What about you?" he asked.

"What do you mean?"

"You seem to care what people think. I mean . . . I get why. The thing with . . . your brother—guys like Chuck saying all that . . . crap. And that's all it is. It's nothing."

"It's easy for you to say that."

"No. It isn't. I just . . . maybe what you're asking is what will they say about . . . the smartest girl in school dancing with a rich-kid flunkie?"

I looked up at him. "I don't think like that."

He raised an eyebrow.

"What?" I said. "I don't."

"Then forget about it. Just for right now. Let's pretend . . ." He grinned. "Pretend we're in kindergarten."

I didn't follow.

"And I just read my best poem . . . to you."

He held out his hand. A little unsure, I stepped back to him, knowing people weren't but fifteen feet from us— laughing and talking. But there I was slow-dancing again with Ricky Martinez under the Texas stars. All the tension in my shoulders eased, and I just let myself be right there. With him. With me. Knowing also that Christina could see me from where she was sitting and she'd really be singing that "Mickey and Ricky sittin' in a tree" song the next day. But that would be tomorrow, and right then—

"Mickey," he said.

"Yeah?" I raised my head from his shoulder.

Then it happened. Not so much as a word. In a look, I leaned in and he leaned in and . . . we kissed. And all those people sitting outside or living it up in the dance fell right out of my mind. There was just this tingling . . . this moment where it was okay to be the girl in the mirror before she tightened her jaw. You'd have thought we were going for the longest softest kiss in history. Maybe we were.

I smiled a lot that night dancing and hanging out with Ricky and not once did it feel fake. Not once did I feel guilty. 'Cause I thought about Dad telling me to "give those boys a break 'cause sometimes they need it." He was right. Sometimes they did.

At some point, we ended up lying on the picnic table talking about all the stars neither one of us knew the names of. So we made up stories about this constellation or that constellation. We didn't see one shooting star, but I made a lot of wishes. Wishes I'd probably have to make come true on my own, but that was okay. Kind of scary but okay.

Eventually it was the four of us sitting together at the

picnic table. Me, Ricky, Christina and Johnny Lee all with our heads tilted back looking up at the sky. We were talking about driving over to the Pizza Hut when all at once I went to thinking about Danny and Roland and something unexpected settled in. That feeling I had in the truck, holding *The Outsiders* after Danny left it in the glove box, swept over me. I understood right then what I couldn't figure out before.

There was something I had to do.

21

The day after the school dance I drove out to the Gonzalez Ranch and sat with Roland's parents. I didn't defend my brother's silence or inability to do what I was doing. I just said how sorry I was for the loss of their son. I'd never said it before. Not without a courtroom and a judge and the desperation of saving Danny. I wasn't trying to save him anymore. I was trying not to hate Roland. Hate him for being eighteen and so full of thinking nothing could've gone wrong. Hate him for making it so that my own brother let him remain the superstar, let him stay gold, even after he died.

Roland's parents stayed pretty quiet. Listening. Smiling some when I told them about the times I'd spent with their son. How he still played the stealing the nose game with his thumb between his fingers when I was already twelve. How he'd throw me up on his shoulders sometimes so I could slam-dunk a basketball in the high school gym. I described a side of Roland that maybe they didn't know. The Roland Gonzalez who really couldn't be understood in a trial or in the headlines for winning state.

It was the hardest thing I'd ever done, sitting with them. It was, as Uncle Jack would've said, the best I could do. The best because Danny was right. Ponyboy does grow up. Not necessarily in the way of wearing a suit and tie or getting married. He grows up in the way that he realizes, like Robert Frost wrote, "nothing gold can stay," but at the same time it can. It can stay gold in your heart even if you gotta let some things go. Especially if you can forgive some things . . . like yourself. I'm still working on that.

One afternoon, I sloshed Dad's truck through the muddy road of The Stick. I crawled up on the hood with *The Outsiders* in my hand. The five o'clock sun glowed, spraying gold across the chattering fields. I folded the cover back and started reading aloud, hoping my voice carried up over the fields, past the stadium, along the highway, and soared right across the Texas state line. I hoped that maybe Danny could hear:

> **When I stepped out into the bright sunlight from the darkness of the movie house, I had only two things on my mind: Paul Newman and a ride home.**

It turned out that Christina was right after all. Danny was famous for something. For being a dad to his son, for being my brother. For being the one who figured out how to stick, in time.

ACKNOWLEDGMENTS

Special thanks to Galen McGriff for being the anchor that you are in my life.

And much gratitude to my swell friends: Patrick Zapata, Shirley Klock, Michael McGriff, Melissa Yurashus, the Milwaukee Chautauqua gals, Lisa Juday, Ruth Schmatz, Mary Stocks, Sarah Miller, Margaret Coble, Jeanette L. Buck, Cheryl Hedrick, Fae Goodman, Robin Cartensen, Sue Mills, Donna Boucher, Howard and Abbie Wells and my family, the Struyfs, EmaLea Mayles, and Paul "Popcorn" Charlton.

No thanks is complete without props to my spectacular editor, Krista Marino, and my wonderful agent, Andrea Cascardi. And thank you to mentors Carolyn Coman, Linda Sanders, Joss Whedon, J. DonLuna, Douglas McGrath, Charles Smith, Alix Olson, and all those striving for excellence at the Highlights Chautauqua Workshop.

Last but by no means least: a most sincere thanks to S. E. Hinton for writing *The Outsiders* and to Sondra McClendon for putting this amazing piece of literature into my hands so many years ago. You both have changed my life forever.

A native South Texan, e.E. Charlton-Trujillo earned a degree in English from Texas A&M Corpus Christi and an MFA in film from Ohio University. Besides being a novelist, she is a playwright, a screenwriter, and an award-winning writer-director of short films.

When she's not writing or filmmaking, she pores over surfing and skateboarding magazines and sneaks in as many episodes of *Buffy the Vampire Slayer* and *Everwood* as she can. Ms. Charlton-Trujillo lives in Madison, Wisconsin. You can visit her at www.bigdreamswrite.com.